The Fight of My Life

By

Lorissa Clemo

MAPLE
PUBLISHERS

The Fight of My Life

Author: Lorissa Clemo

Copyright © Lorissa Clemo (2022)

The right of Lorissa Clemo to be identified as author of this work has been asserted by the author in accordance with section 77 and 78 of the Copyright, Designs and Patents Act 1988.

First Published in 2022

ISBN 978-1-915492-71-5 (Paperback)
       978-1-915492-72-2 (E-Book)

Book cover design and Book layout by:
    Maple Publishers
    www.maplepublishers.com

Published by:
    Maple Publishers
    1 Brunel Way,
    Slough,
    SL1 1FQ, UK
    www.maplepublishers.com

A CIP catalogue record for this title is available from the British Library.

I have spent most of my life dreaming of finding my soul mate. My one true love. By the time I was 25 I had been in a few relationships but nothing was ever completely right. I would be happy for a while but I would soon realise that they weren't the one for me. The last relationship I was in, lasted 3 years and made me give up on my dream. He was the furthest away from being a gentleman anyone could get. If only I had left sooner. This relationship is my biggest regret.

I was 22 when I met him. On a night out with my girlfriend's I noticed him across the dancefloor and as he noticed me, I blushed. He was so handsome.

"I would never have a chance with him." I thought to myself.

I carried on dancing with my friends and forgot all about him. That was until I was getting myself a drink at the bar. I felt a tap on my shoulder and I turned around thinking it was one of my friends. But it was him. I smiled at him and he smiled back.

"Can I buy you a drink?" he shouted over the loud music.

I nodded and he ordered 2 bottles of cider. My friends were busy dancing so this handsome stranger and I went to find somewhere to sit and talk.

"Hi, my name is Ian." He shouted as he leaned in so I could hear.

"Hi Ian. I'm Amanda." I shouted back.

We sat there for a while, getting to know each other. Eventually, my friends came looking for me, and as they found me they came bouncing over to us. As they grabbed my arm and pulled me away, I waved goodbye to Ian, hoping

I would see him again. I spent the rest of the night thinking about him. The night went on and at closing time we all left, I hadn't seen Ian again so I was a bit disappointed. But as we got outside he was there waiting. Instantly a big smile spread across my face.

"Hi Amanda. I was really hoping you hadn't left early." he said, smiling.

He had such a gorgeous smile. We stood together talking while my friends sorted a taxi home.

"What's your phone number?" he asked, handing me his phone.

I put my number in and turned to walk away, I couldn't help smiling.

"So, who was that?" asked my friend, Hannah.

"He's called Ian. He seems really nice. And he's so handsome." I replied.

"Oh, honey. He's drop dead gorgeous. And you both looked great together." Another friend squealed.

"Oh stop it, Kelly." I said, giggling.

Now I just had to wait and see if I would hear from him. Over the next few days I carried on with my life and eventually, I heard from him.

"Hi Amanda. Sorry it's taken so long to get in touch. Would you like to go out to dinner some time soon?" the message read.

I was so happy. He wanted to meet! As I typed out my reply, agreeing to a dinner date I was so excited. We spent the rest of the day messaging each other. We had arranged to meet for dinner that weekend so I decided to go shopping and pick out a new outfit for the occasion. When Saturday arrived, I spent the day preparing myself, physically and mentally for our date. He was picking me up and we went to a nice pub. We ordered our drinks and sat down at a table together. We talked for hours about all sorts of things. Our lives, what we liked and didn't like. It was a wonderful evening. And after that night we were inseparable. On the rare occasions that we weren't together, we would be messaging or calling each other all the time. He was so sweet and would say the most amazing things to me. Every morning I would wake up to a message from him.

"Good morning beautiful!" always the same but it always put a smile on my face.

We spent so much time together and after a month we were officially a couple. I was the happiest I had ever been and so was Ian. All of our free time was spent together. We went to the beach, went on long walks, visited some really lovely places and sometimes we just sat and watched films. It was amazing to have someone in my life who actually wanted to spend so much time with me. He made me laugh, he complimented me all the time, he made me smile when I felt sad, and he was so handsome. I had never been so happy.

We had been together 6 months and we had started to discuss living together. We were so in love and wanted to be with each other all the time. So we decided to see if we could find somewhere to live together. After looking for a month all the time we found a cute 3 bedroom house to rent. It was perfect for us. Eventually we moved in and I was so excited. Little did I know it would turn into a nightmare.

At first we were so happy. It may not of been ours, but we were together. We had been living there for about

3 weeks when he invited his best friend, Ryan, over. They both had quite a bit to drink, and then the first argument began. I don't really know how it started, but it ended with me sat, alone in the bedroom, crying.

"You will never be anything like my ex!" he shouted at me as he slammed the door shut.

Looking back now that was the first red flag. I should of left then but even then I blamed it on the fact he was drunk, that he didn't mean it. The next day everything was back to normal, as if he hadn't said something so mean the night before. For a while things were good again, I was sure it was a one off. And soon enough things took a turn for the worse again. We were planning on seeing his family at the weekend but with both of us working all week, jobs at home hadn't been done. So I decided I would stay home and clean.

"But you said you would come with me!" he shouted.

I didn't understand why he was so upset. He never spent time with my family and it wasn't as if I didn't want to go. The house needed a good clean. He looked at me in a way no one had ever looked at me before. Like he hated me. If looks could kill, I would of died right there. In the end I gave in and did what he wanted. Even though he got his own way, he still sulked for the rest of the day. Promising we would spend the afternoon together after seeing his parents, we left and drove to see them. However, we ended up being there all day. He was happy to have seen and spent time with them and I was happy for him. When we returned home I got on with housework while he cracked open the first of many beers. In the end we had a nice relaxing evening and sat and watched a film together. He had drunk about 5 cans of beer and fallen asleep on the sofa. He had previously told me that if he does, try to wake him up and get him to go to bed. So that is what I did. I began by shaking him gently, which didn't work. I tried again to wake him and eventually I managed to. But instead of just going to bed, he shouted at me.

"Why did you wake me up? Leave me alone!" and with that he rolled over and ignored me.

I decided to just go to bed and leave him there. But in the morning the argument would begin again.

"I slept on the sofa most of the night! Why didn't you wake me up?" he screamed at me.

I was shocked.

"I tried to wake you." I explained.

He was so mad at me and then he started with the name calling.

"You're so stupid. How could you think I would want to sleep on the sofa all night?" he shouted.

Before I could say anything, he turned and went to sit in the garden. I stood in the living room, not really knowing what was happening. When he eventually came back inside I tried to apologise to him, but he just walked straight past me, got ready for work and left, not saying a word. I spent all day thinking about that morning. I wanted to make it up to him so I decided to cook his favourite meal for tea, lasagne. He would normally be home around 6pm so I thought I would have it ready for 6.30pm. But he never showed up. I tried phoning him but he was ignoring my calls. I was starting to get worried. But eventually, at 10pm he finally arrived home.

"Where have been? I was getting really worried. I cooked your favourite meal and now it's ruined." I told him.

"Well I didn't want to come home after this morning. I'm going for a shower and then to bed." he said angrily as he stormed past me.

I didn't know what to do. All I had wanted to do all day was to apologise for the night before. He locked himself in the bathroom, so I just went to bed, upset. By the time he got into bed I was fast asleep.

In the morning I was worried he would still be upset with me. But he wasn't. He was back to being his normal self again. He woke up and got ready for work, kissing me on the forehead before he left. I was so confused, we had argued but sorted nothing. For the next few days everything was normal again. He was loving, happy and spent time with me. However, he turned again and said some more horrible things.

"I'm going to stay with my parents over the weekend and spend some time with them." I explained.

"Oh, what so you can see your other boyfriend? You slag!" he snarled.

I was completely shocked. Why would he say something like that?

"What? Why would you say that? I'm just going to be with my family." I tried explaining to him.

"No you won't! You will be with your other man!"

He made me feel so bad about seeing them. We ended up arguing for hours. Then all of a sudden Ian picked up my empty mug and threw it across the room. It smashed to pieces and he just sat back down on the sofa, laughing at me. I had a lump in my throat and I could feel the tears rolling down my face. I stood up and went to clean the mess, but I was so shocked I wasn't concentrating and cut myself on the broken mug. Ian didn't care though, he just sat there, pretending I wasn't there. We spent the rest of the evening not talking to each other. I couldn't believe I had upset him again. In my head I was punishing myself.

"I'm so stupid." I would think to myself.

I decided to leave him there and I went to bed. As I stood up I said softly,

"I won't go at the weekend. But I am going to bed now. Goodnight."

As I walked away I was sure I saw him smirk. I got into bed and cried myself to sleep. The next day he was back to his normal self again. Now I can see that was because he got his own way and I wouldn't see my family. I would spend the weekend with him. I was upset that I wasn't going to see my family. I had to make up a reason why I couldn't see them.

"Hi mum. Sorry I can't make it over at the weekend. I have been asked to work. I'm really sorry."

"That's okay honey. We can do something else soon." Mum replied.

We spoke on the phone for a while, talking about all sorts. And as we said goodbye, a tear rolled down my cheek, and hanging up, I sat and cried. I knew that I would of had a lovely time with them and I knew now Ian and I weren't going to do anything but just sit and watch the telly or films.

Over the next few weeks he was back to being loving again. He would tell me about his day and I would tell him about mine. We even went out over the weekends, which was lovely. But on one Sunday afternoon I suggested going to our local pub for some food and a drink. He said that would be nice, so off we went. When we got there it was busy but there were a couple of people there that Ian knew, so we stood at the bar with them. I had no idea who these people were and as Ian spoke to them he completely ignored me. No one bothered to talk to me at all. I tried my best to be involved in the conversation, but it was useless. I just stood there, listening to what they were saying, drinking and wishing to go home. I knew it was my idea to go but with no one making any effort to include me, I just didn't want to be there anymore. Eventually, we left and went home and I decided to head straight to bed. I couldn't believe I had been ignored all evening.

"What's wrong with you?" he barked.

"Well it wasn't very nice to be ignored all evening." I explained, timidly.

"You wanted to go out. It's not my fault you didn't speak." He said angrily.

He always made me believe that it was me, that I was the problem. I lay in bed thinking about everything. I knew that he was angry with me now, but I also knew that everything would be back to normal a couple of days later. After that evening, we had a couple of nice evenings together again, but then the name calling began again. He started calling me a retard and calling me stupid. It was happening more and more often. Of course there where plenty of times I tried to leave him, but he would apologise and cry and he always said that he would kill himself if I left him. I felt completely trapped in this relationship. Sometimes in the middle of an argument, he would get in the car and drive off. Then he would phone me and tell me he was going to jump off a bridge. It terrified me every time, so I would beg him to come home and hours later, he would finally stroll through the door. As he walked through the door I would let out a huge sigh of relief, but Ian would look at me with hate in his eyes. He stormed past me to go to bed, without saying a word.

I was walking on eggshells all the time, but after a few days he was talking to me again.

"Shall we do something nice this weekend? Maybe a walk and picnic?" he asked.

"Umm, yeah. Sounds lovely." I replied, hoping that it genuinely would be lovely.

That weekend we went out together along a gorgeous coastal path. It was really beautiful. We walked and talked together and sat on the beach and had a wonderful picnic. It really was a fantastic day. I was so happy. And Ian looked really happy too. This happiness lasted quite a while. Ian would actually spend time with me and he was coming home at a normal and decent time. We were actually a happy couple. But, of course, it didn't last. I had hoped with all my heart that it would last, but again the arguments began.

"Why are you looking at me like that? I have just walked through the door!" he snapped.

"Like what? I have literally just asked if you have had a good day! What do you mean?" I asked, nervously.

He slammed the door shut and stormed into the kitchen, grabbed a beer and sat on the sofa, looking at me in disgust. I sat there not knowing what to say. I tried to speak to him, ask about his day again.

"How was work then?" I asked softly.

"DON'T TALK TO ME!" he shouted, angrily.

He had his phone in his hand and as he shouted at me, he threw his phone across the room, smashing the screen so much that the background picture was totally unrecognisable. It was completely broken.

"Look what you made me do! You have broken my phone!" he screamed.

I was totally gobsmacked. I didn't know what to say, he got up and went and sat in the garden for what seemed like forever. Coming back inside he was so angry, he sat on the sofa next to me and laughed.

"How did I make you throw your phone? I didn't do anything."

"God you're so stupid. It's all your fault. Everything is your fault. You haven't even cooked me anything."

"What would you like? I'll go make you something." I told him, now feeling bad that I hadn't cooked anything. It was gone 9'o'clock in the evening though.

"No! I just won't eat anything now!" he said, cracking open another beer.

We spent the rest of the evening in silence. By the time I had decided to go to bed, Ian had fallen asleep on the sofa. I made the decision to leave him there. He was already mad at me so I thought I would just deal with it in the morning. But in the morning he didn't say anything to me. I was up and getting ready for work before he had woken up. When he did eventually surface, he just left for work, without saying a word. I was already dreading him coming home, I was sure there would be another argument. And I was right.

When he did finally arrive home, he was now mad that I didn't have tea ready and on the table for him, and that I had already eaten. He didn't get home till half 11 that night though!

"Why haven't you made me anything for tea?" he barked at me.

"Well I never know when you're going to be home. Last time I made you something you were really late home." I tried explaining.

"Well, go make me something while I go for a bath!" he ordered as he stormed off, slamming the door behind him.

The weeks went by and they were a mix of good and bad. And as Christmas finally came around I began to get really excited. Christmas is my favourite time of year. I love buying gifts for all the important people in my life, and I love seeing their reactions. Ian and I eventually decided to spend Christmas day with my family and boxing day with his family. I was really surprised that he was actually willing to spend some time with my family. My parents got us a joint gift of a nights stay at a really lovely hotel. It sounded amazing. A 3 course meal, breakfast and a glass of prosecco on arrival. We were both really looking forward to it. Maybe a little break away was just what we needed. My parents also bought Ian a gift card for a clothes shop that he liked. Ian seemed to actually be grateful and looked like he was enjoying himself. We played several different board games and had a really lovely time all together. But it was soon time to leave again. I hated leaving them. Especially because I would never know what kind of mood Ian would be in when we left. As we left, a tear rolled down my cheek. I didn't want it to end. And unlucky for me, Ian's mood changed.

"I wanted to leave earlier. We have been there way too long. God you're so thick. Could you not tell I wanted to leave?" he said, angrily.

"I'm sorry. No I didn't. But it was really great spending some time with them, wasn't it?" I asked.

"It was fine." and with that he drove away.

The whole journey home, we didn't say anything to each other. Luckily the radio was on so I was just listening to that. I couldn't believe that he was mad at me yet again. I was starting to feel very depressed about the relationship. I always seemed to be doing something wrong, and I always felt bad.

"I'm so stupid!" I thought to myself on the way home.

When we did eventually get home he was still in a bad mood with me. I got out of the car and he just sat there.

"Aren't you coming inside?" I asked him, softly.

"No! I'm going to sit here for a while. Leave me alone!"

I didn't think too much of him staying sat in the car. He was mad at me again and he would rather sit alone, instead of talking to me about it. So I went inside and went for a shower. Eventually, after about an hour and a half he came inside. When he sat down next to me he smelt completely different. It took me a few minutes to realise what it was. Weed.

"Have you just been smoking weed?" I asked him.

"Of course not! Why would you even ask that?" he replied.

"Well you smell like it. I know what it smells like."

"You obviously don't because I haven't smoked it in years."

With that he grabbed a beer and looked at me with that evil look in his eyes.

"You really are thick, aren't you?" Ian snarled.

I sat there for a while, in silence. He totally ignored me and I didn't know what to say to him. Whatever I said would if resulted in him screaming and shouting at me. So I stayed quiet. After he opened his 8th beer that evening I decided to go to bed. I knew the more he drank, the more likely it was that we would argue.

"I'm going to bed now. I'll see you in the morning." I said looking at him, wondering if I should kiss him goodnight or not.

"Fine!" he replied.

He obviously didn't want a kiss so I just made my way up to bed.

"You ruined a perfectly nice day." He shouted at me as I climbed the stairs to bed.

As I got into bed I curled up in a ball and cried. Was it really my fault? Had I really ruined our day? I must of. I hoped that Ian would fall asleep on the sofa. I just wanted to be alone. It was another night that I cried myself to sleep.

The next morning Ian was back to his happy self. After all he was going to see his family. We had a good day and everyone enjoyed themselves. We had a lovely Christmas dinner and had lots of laughs. It was definitely a better day than I had expected it to be, but I was just happy to see Ian happy.

The next few days were really lovely between Ian and I and we had enjoyed each others company. I had almost forgotten that he could be so mean. Almost! By New Year's Eve he was back to being horrible. I had been food shopping for party food because we had some of his friends coming over to see in the New Year. But he said I shouldn't be wasting money.

"You have spent so much on just one evening. Next time ask me!" he ordered.

Now he was watching how much I spent? But I had my own job. I had my own money. Why was he now being like this about money?

From then on I always had to ask him before I spent any money at all. Even my own money. That wasn't the only thing that changed. He started demanding to look at my phone. It soon became a daily thing, like the smoking of weed and lying about it. The name calling got worse. Of course, I still thought about leaving, but every time I tried, he would guilt me into staying.

"I'll go jump off a bridge if you leave me!" he would cry to me.

He would sit on the floor, crying, shouting and screaming at me. Telling me it was all my fault. His depression was my fault and the more he said it, the more I believed it. I started to become depressed and my job wasn't helping. Working in retail could be really difficult, but trying to get through a shift after an argument with Ian was even harder. My colleagues knew something was wrong but I couldn't tell them. It was all my fault after all, and they would say the same. I didn't need to hear it from anyone else, I heard it enough from Ian. The more depressed I became, the more

I thought about talking to Ian about it all. After all he had suffered for a long time too. So one evening, when he wasn't shouting at me, I decided to see if we could talk about it. But I should of known that was a mistake.

"Ian, honey. Could we sit and have a chat please? I've been feeling really low lately." I asked him quietly.

"Yeah, of course. What's wrong?"

I have to admit, I was surprised but it wouldn't last long. I started to explain how I had been feeling and he soon twisted it all around to be all about him. How he was so much more depressed than me. As I carried on trying to explain, he would interrupt me and wouldn't listen to anything that I was saying. In the end I just stopped talking and just listened to him. He talked about himself for what seemed to be forever and he didn't ask me anything. He just talked at me for hours. And of course it turned into an argument. He started shouting at me again.

"You! You are the reason. God you are so annoying and it's all your fault." He cried, as he left to sit in the garden.

I was stunned. Yet again he twisted everything round and made me feel so much guilt for just trying to talk to him. Over the next few days he seemed to be in a good mood. He was actually smiling and we weren't arguing. It was so nice to not have him shouting at me all the time. I wondered how long it would last. Our night away was only a few weeks away and I was now starting to look forward to it, but I was also dreading Ian being in a foul mood. I prayed that this current good mood of his was going to last. I wasn't sure it would as they never lasted long, but if it lasted I was sure we would have a great time.

Eventually it was time for our mini break and Ian was still in a really good mood. We were both looking forward to spending some quality time together. When we finally arrived at the hotel we were shown to our room and it was beautiful. There was a bottle of prosecco chilling in an ice bucket so we opened it and toasted to us.

"To us! Let's both have a wonderful time!" Ian said, smiling and raising his glass.

We sat and talked together, laughing with each other. We drank the bottle of prosecco and it was soon time for our meal at a restaurant just up the road from our hotel. We strolled to the restaurant and as we arrived we were shown to our table. We hadn't done anything like that for months and it was really lovely. To begin with. It didn't last long. The server bought two glasses of wine over to our table and we looked through the menu.

"This is an awful menu. There isn't anything here I will like!" Ian snapped.

He looked at me as if it was my fault.

"Why did your parents book this place? I don't like the sound of anything here."

He put down his menu, picked up his wine glass and finished his drink. The server came back to ask if we were ready to order and Ian looked at him as if the server had asked the most ridiculous question you could think of.

"No! We are not ready. But I will have a pint!" Ian ordered.

The server walked away and I whispered,

"Did you have to be so rude?"

He just shrugged his shoulders and picked up his menu again. Finally he decided on a steak dish and when the food arrived I thought it looked amazing. However, Ian didn't think so. He had a couple bites of his meal and left the rest. He barely spoke to me the whole time we were there. The meal had been ruined. He was quite happy to drink as much beer as he could though. By the time we had finished our meals Ian was in a bad mood and I was upset. As we walked back to the hotel his mood seemed to lift again and as we arrived back we decided to have a couple of drinks at the bar before heading back to our room. We talked and laughed together, had a couple of drinks and made our way back to our room. As we sat together on the bed we decided to watch a film and cuddle in bed. Ian started to make a move, he kissed me passionately and went to take my top off. I kissed him back and told him I just needed to go to the bathroom first.

"Are you serious?" he shouted.

"You are so selfish. Such a selfish bitch."

I was shaking so much. I tried to explain that I wasn't pushing him away, but he wasn't having any of it. He just wouldn't listen.

"You saving yourself for your other boyfriend? You slag!" and with that he locked himself in the bathroom.

"I'm sorry!" I said, as I sobbed.

"No you're not! You have ruined everything!" he shouted back at me through the door.

He stayed in the bathroom for what seemed like forever. I was sat on the bed, crying into the pillow.

"I'm so stupid!" I thought to myself.

Eventually he opened the door. I jumped off the bed and rushed over to him to apologise again. What came next

I never imagined would happen. I stood in front of him, saying sorry. Then he pushed me really hard into the corner of the chest of drawers. He didn't care that he had hurt me, he just climbed into bed, rolled over and didn't say anything to me. I stood, holding onto my hip. I was certain it would bruise. I was in total shock, I just didn't know what to do. We were meant to be exploring the city the next day but I just wanted to go home. I sat on the floor for a while, still sobbing quietly. When Ian had fallen asleep I climbed into bed next to him. Eventually I managed to fall asleep. I had nightmares all night of him shoving me into the drawers and I kept waking up all night. Ian slept all night and in the morning seemed to be normal again. Had he forgotten what had happened last night? We left to go down for our breakfast and sat down at a table. The first thing Ian did was take his phone out of his pocket and he just sat on his phone the whole time. I tried to make conversation, but it was like talking to a brick wall. After breakfast we walked silently back to our room.

"Well today is going to be awful." I thought to myself.

We got ready for our day out together and I was dreading it, but all of a sudden he started smiling and began talking about our day out. He genuinely sounded excited. So we both left the hotel, hand in hand. I was so scared that he would end up in a bad mood that I just said that we would do whatever he wanted to do. Surely then, if it turns out to be a bad day it wouldn't be my fault. We walked around the city hand in hand and had a really lovely time together. We decided to stop in a pub and have a drink. We ordered a cocktail each and sat down at a table. It was a really lovely place, and we talked for hours. We had a wonderful time laughing and joking.

"I love you!" he whispered while looking me directly in the eyes.

I was completely gobsmacked. After the previous night I was sure he didn't love me.

"I love you too." I whispered back.

We stayed in the pub for a while and decided to order some lunch. The food was amazing and we continued to laugh and joke with each other. I was so glad that we were having a good day. After lunch we carried on walking around the city and did a little bit of shopping. Later in the afternoon we made our way home.

As the weeks passed we continued to be the happy couple I had hoped and dreamed we could be. We were both really happy and always saying "I love you" to each other. Sometimes my mind would go back to that night at the hotel, but I would try and forget about it. I would tell myself it was a one off. A month after our hotel stay, Ian came home from work with a huge smile on his face.

"What's got you so happy?" I asked.

"I have a surprise for you!" he replied with excitement.

"Close your eyes!"

I closed my eyes, wondering what it could possibly be. That's when I heard footsteps, but they weren't Ian's. A dog? As I opened my eyes there was a springer spaniel bouncing through the living room.

"Oh my god! A dog?" I exclaimed.

"This is Daisy. She really needs a new home. So, here she is!"

"She's so beautiful." I squealed as she came bounding over to me.

Daisy was a white and liver springer and she was 3 years old. Ian rescued her. She was a little bit on the round side but we would soon get her down to a good weight for her size. Daisy soon became my best friend, and I loved her dearly. For weeks, Ian and Daisy and I would spend every Sunday together going for lovely long walks and Ian and I had been really enjoying each others company. Things were great and I was happy. I hoped that this feeling would last and I really believed that it could. One Sunday we decided to go into the city and do some shopping. We left Daisy with Ian's parents and we drove off for our shopping trip. Ian had decided to take the gift card he got from my parents so he could treat himself to some new clothes. We had a nice time together and had lunch in a cute little restaurant.

"Thank you for a lovely day!" I said with a smile as we drove back to his parents to pick up Daisy.

"It's okay. It was a good day. We will stay at my parents for a while okay. Maybe an hour." Ian told me.

When we arrived, Daisy came bouncing up to both of us. She was so happy to see us, and I was happy to see her. I gave her a cuddle and sat with Ian's mum. We talked for a while and eventually, after 2 hours, we left for home.

"Shall we take Daisy for a walk before we go home?" I asked him.

"Yeah we can take her up to the field for a run around." He replied.

The field was just up the road from where we lived, and Daisy could run around like the crazy dog she was and she loved it. We finally arrived home and we all sat on the sofa deciding what to have for tea.

"What do you want me to cook?" I asked.

"Its okay, I will order us a pizza."

"I don't mind cooking. We had takeaway last night."

As I told him his face turned from happy and smiling to anger and hatred. Instantly regretting what I said, I knew we were about to have an argument.

"Are you serious? I said I will order a pizza?!" he snarled.

He stomped around the house in anger and I just sat on the sofa with tears in my eyes.

"You have ruined a lovely day!" he shouted as he stormed out of the house.

I heard the car start and that was it, he had driven away. I didn't know what to do. Daisy didn't like the shouting, so had taken herself upstairs to hide. So I sat there, alone. It wasn't long until I started to worry about him.

"What is he doing? Where has he gone?" I thought to myself.

He could of gone anywhere and I didn't know where to begin looking for him. So I rang him instead. He answered the phone, and for a moment I was relieved.

"What?" he said, bluntly.

"I'm sorry! We will order a pizza. I was just…"

"Oh, shut up! You're so pathetic and stupid. Such a retard. I'm not hungry anymore so don't bother!"

Ian hung up the phone leaving those words ringing in my ears. I was really worried about him and that he would do something stupid. He had threatened to take his own life multiple times. I tried calling him again but he just ignored it. I was getting more and more worried. Eventually, 4 hours after he left, he arrived home.

"You're back!" I said, tears rolling down my face, as I stood up to give him a hug.

"Get off me!" he snarled.

Walking straight past me he looked at me with anger and hatred in his eyes.

"I'm going to bed, so just leave me alone!"

He stomped up the stairs leaving me stood there. Poor Daisy came running downstairs to get away from him. Even she couldn't stand his bad moods. Daisy and I sat together and I could hear Ian stomping around upstairs. I was wondering what on earth he was doing and about 2 minutes later he came back downstairs carrying the jumper he bought with the voucher my parents gave him.

"This is what I think of today!" he snarled.

Opening the log burner, he threw the jumper inside and marched back upstairs and got into bed. I just sat, watching the jumper burn. I never imagined he could do something like that. I was so angry and upset, but I knew I couldn't say anything to him. I spent the night on he sofa, too scared to go upstairs, and Daisy spent the night cuddled up with me. I could tell she was sad and she could tell I was too. The next morning I woke up early and tip-toed upstairs to get changed and Ian was still asleep. As I tip-toed back downstairs I heard him starting to wake up. He stomped around upstairs getting ready for work and I knew he was still angry at me. He came flying down the stairs and into the living room, not saying a word to me, he put on his work boots.

"Morning." I said, timidly.

He just looked at me and left for work. Daisy had gone back upstairs again to hide and I just stayed sat on the sofa. I was upset and angry at him and he was with me. I was already dreading him coming home from work that evening. I decided to do some housework and take Daisy for a nice long walk and hopefully clear my head. Hopefully he would of calmed down by the time he would finish work. I spent the day worrying about what type of mood he would be in when he did finally get home. Eventually, at 10pm he strolled through the door. He looked me in the eyes and said,

"Sorry I'm really late back but it's been a really busy day."

"It's okay. I hope it's been a good day though." I replied as he kissed me.

I was totally surprised, but happy he was finally back to being in a good mood. We sat together and talked in a way we hadn't for ages. We were happy and cuddled up with each other and Daisy was lying beside us. As I decided to head up to bed I said goodnight to Ian and strolled up to bed with a smile on my face, finally. I fell asleep having enjoyed our evening together.

Over the next few months we were both really happy and enjoying each others company. We were even going out together with Daisy at the weekends. Life finally felt good and I was starting to believe that Ian might actually love me. The arguments had stopped and he was always smiling. My birthday was fast approaching and all I wished for was for this relationship bliss to continue. On the day of my birthday Ian surprised me with a lovely bunch of flowers and breakfast in bed before heading downstairs for my presents.

"Happy birthday baby!" he exclaimed as he got back into bed with me for breakfast. He had made pancakes which had syrup all over them and a cup of tea.

"Thank you. This looks amazing!" I replied.

"That's okay baby. It took me ages to sort all of this for you." He told me.

He kissed me on the cheek and we sat and ate breakfast and then wondered downstairs. We sat down for me to open my presents. I had already clocked the huge present on the other side of the room, and I couldn't wait to see what it was. But first he handed me a card and said,

"We will do whatever you like today. Anything you like." He smiled at me and handed me the card.

Inside the card he had written.

"To my beautiful girlfriend, happy birthday! I love you more than words could ever say. Ian."

He looked at me with love in his eyes for the first time in a long time and I smiled. We felt like a real couple, finally. And with that, I knew what I wanted to do.

"Let's go to a nice quiet woods somewhere, with a river so we can all go for a little swim. Somewhere nice and peaceful. We could also take a picnic. It's a glorious day and I think we should make the most of it."

"Sounds like a great idea. We shall do that!" he smiled and handed me a gift bag.

Excitedly, I opened the bag and peered inside. 2 bottles of gin and what looked like a jewellery box. I opened the box and inside was a gorgeous, silver necklace.

"Thank you so much." I said as I gave him a kiss.

"It's okay. Now for that one!" he pointed to the huge present across the room.

Wondering what it could possibly be, I tore through the wrapping paper to uncover a garden wishing well. The only problem was, it looked half finished.

"I made it for you with my dad. Do you like it? I'm sorry it's not completely finished, I've been busy at work but we will finish it. I promise." He explained.

"Yeah. It will look great in the garden." I told him, trying to convince myself that he would actually finish it.

After I had opened my cards and gifts we started to get ready to head to a beautiful quiet woods we knew that wasn't too far away. I was so happy and looking forward to a great day out. Daisy was running around the house excitedly as if she knew where we were going.

Finally we were ready to leave. We had our picnic all sorted and Daisy was ready to go. As we left the house, Ian pulled me close to him, kissed me and whispered in my ear,

"We will have an amazing day together. Happy birthday baby."

I walked out with a smile on my face. I was so happy, and it felt amazing. It was my birthday and Ian was being so loving. We had a fantastic time out and Daisy loved running around and jumping in the river. She was such a water dog. We spent all day in the woods. Swimming, sitting in the sun, just really enjoying each others company.

"Right baby. It's time to head home. I have one more surprise for you." Ian declared.

"Really? What is it?" I asked.

"You will have to wait and see, but we just need to pop to my parents so they can look after Daisy for us." he explained.

I couldn't help but wonder what our evening plans were. And as Ian pulled me to my feet I smiled sweetly at him. And with that we left for his parents house and as we drove over I thought to myself,

"Today has been amazing! Ian has been in a good mood and there hasn't been a single argument. I don't want today to end. He is amazing."

We went into his parents house and sat and had a chat before leaving Daisy there and heading home.

"Right baby. We will head home to get ready and then I'm taking you out for a nice birthday meal." he told me with a grin on his face.

I was so excited and happy. We had had a wonderful day and it was going to be a wonderful evening too. With Ian sat beside me, we both smiled and made our way home. When we arrived home Ian turned to me, looking me in the eyes and said,

"Now go and get ready for a fantastic evening. Put on a nice dress and some heels. Be ready in an hour."

Giddy with excitement, I ran upstairs and jumped straight in the shower. I put on some music and sang along, terribly, but smiling from ear to ear. Once I had showered I skipped into the bedroom to choose a dress and heels. Pulling everything out of my wardrobe I found a gorgeous, little black dress that I hadn't worn for a long time. Praying that it would still fit , I slipped into it. I curled my long, blonde hair and put on some subtle make up and put on a pair of strappy, black heels. Ian was downstairs, waiting for me and as I walked down the stairs he was stood in the living room with a bunch of flowers.

"Wow! Baby you look amazing! So beautiful." He exclaimed.

Blushing, I thanked him and he handed me the flowers. He rarely bought me flowers or told me that I looked beautiful so these little things really made me happy.

"Lillies. Thank you. I love them."

I put the Lillie's in some water and we left for the restaurant. About 30 minutes later we arrived, and it looked amazing. It looked like an incredibly romantic place. Candles on the tables, soft, romantic music playing in the background and all the tables were setup for two people.

"Wow! This place looks incredible! So romantic." I whispered.

"It took me a while to find this place but I'm so glad that I found it. Let's go inside and have a drink before our reservation." he told me.

We stepped inside and the host welcomed us. She showed us to the bar where we could sit for 20 minutes until our table was ready. We sat there and talked and laughed together. I couldn't stop smiling. Finally our table was ready and as we walked over I couldn't help noticing how handsome Ian looked. He was smiling and he was genuinely happy for the first time in a long time. Ian pulled my chair out and as I sat down he kissed the top of my head.

"Tonight is going to be amazing." I thought to myself.

We ordered a bottle of wine and our food and carried on talking. We talked about all sorts. Our jobs, what we wanted out of life, our families, and so much more. We laughed and joked so much, we were only quiet when we were eating. The food came out and it looked amazing and tasted even better. We decided to get a dessert to share and we had some more drink. When we finished our meal, Ian grabbed my hand and looked deep into my eyes.

"I hope you have had a fantastic birthday. I love you." he said, softly.

And with that Ian got up and gave me a kiss. The sun was starting to set so we thought it would be nice to watch the sunset on a nearby beach. The perfect way to end the perfect day.

Over the next few weeks we spent lots of time together and enjoying each others company. It was in these times I didn't want to leave him. In these moments I was genuinely happy and felt like Ian actually, maybe, did love me. He made time for me and we would talk and laugh with each other. Daisy was happy too. She would snuggle up between us in the evenings and fall asleep while Ian and I watched a film. Everything seemed to be perfect. Or so I thought. One Saturday evening we went to our local pub and had a nice meal and a few drinks. We had a really lovely time until we returned home. Ian continued to drink and soon had too much and got cross at me for no reason.

"Leave me alone, you psycho!" he yelled.

He rolled over on the sofa and within 2 minutes, he was asleep. Now, I don't know why I did it, or why I thought it was a good idea but I looked through his phone. I had never done that before, never even thought about it. I guess that even though he always had his phone on him it just never crossed my mind. But there were a lot of messages to and from a lot of other girls. All of these messages started with him, being crude. Some of the girls weren't interested and made that clear, but others replied and arranged to meet him. My jaw hit the floor! These messages were definitely not from friends . I thought I could trust him. I scrolled through the long list of girls and got angrier and angrier. I knew I had to confront him but I was terrified. I knew it would turn into a massive argument. But I had to do it. Nervously, I woke him up and he could tell I was upset and angry about something.

"What? Why have you woken me up?" he snapped.

"We need to talk! Who are all these girls and why are you sending them sexual messages?" I asked angrily.

He looked at me with a dirty look in his eyes and laughed.

"So you have been through my phone? Not trust me?" Ian laughed, trying to make me feel bad.

"I just looked. But why should I trust you when you're sending those kind of messages to loads of other girls?"

Ian burst into laughter, it was almost evil.

"It was a joke! Can you not take a joke?" he snarled.

I looked him in the eyes, knowing he was lying. Knowing he was about to make me believe that I was crazy. I was convinced that he had cheated at this point. But there was no way he was going to make himself look bad. So instead, he made me feel bad and that I was the only one in the wrong.

"People don't make those kind of jokes to people they don't know. It's not funny!" I tried explaining to him.

"Oh my god! I'm not a slag like you! I was joking!" he shouted as he stormed out, throwing a mug as he left.

Ian was the one in the wrong, but I was the one that felt incredibly bad. Daisy had already ran upstairs to hide and so I was left on the sofa, angry and upset. Ian had walked off and I had no idea where he went. So I cleaned up the mess from him throwing a mug. Cleaned up the tea on the walls, picked up all the pieces of the broken mug. Sobbing for hours I sat alone, wondering where he was and when he would be back. Eventually, I decided to climb into bed and lie there with Daisy. We lay there together for what seemed like hours before we heard him walk up the drive. My heart started pounding. I was shaking and Daisy had jumped off the bed and found somewhere to hide. Ian stormed through the front door, slamming the door behind him. I heard him stomp around downstairs, kicking off his shoes and opening another can of beer. He stumbled up the stairs and clambered into bed next to me, without saying a word and practically fell asleep instantly, not without shoving me first though. I lay in bed wide awake for hours with him snoring beside me. In the end I drifted off to sleep.

As morning came around and I started to wake up, I noticed Daisy sleeping soundly on the floor next to me. Ian was still fast asleep and would be for at least another hour. So I sneaked past Daisy and out of the bedroom door. I was dreading Ian waking up and starting another argument, but I was still so cross with him. I knew that I couldn't mention the messages again.

"Maybe he *was* just joking with all those girls?" I thought to myself.

I started to get myself ready for work and tidy up Ian's mess in the living room and by the time that was done and I was ready, he had finally started to wake up. I knew he was still in a bad mood by all the stomping around and the fact that Daisy came running down the stairs. When he did finally come downstairs he did his usual, put his boots on, gave me an evil look and left for work without saying a word. I carried on getting ready for work and left, knowing that this would carry on into the evening. All day at work all I could think about were all the messages to all the different girls. Playing the previous night over and over again in my head.

After a long day at work I arrived home with no sign of Ian. Nothing new there. I got myself showered and started making my tea, wondering what time he would arrive home. By the time I sat down with my tea it was half past six. I sat and watched rubbish on the telly for hours, and by the time Ian came home it was 11pm. He walked through the door with a face like thunder and instantly my heart started beating really fast. I stayed glued to the sofa waiting to see if he would say anything. He walked past me and straight into the kitchen and grabbed a beer, looking at me in such an angry way. I decided I would try and say something and see I could get some sort of conversation out of him.

"How was your day?" I asked timidly.

"Just don't talk to me! I am going to sit here, watch what I want and drink beer." he replied.

I didn't want another shouting match so I just sat there and kept my mouth shut. We both sat there with Daisy between us, Ian drinking and I just watched whatever rubbish he had put on the telly. He drank beer after beer and soon the looks of hatred began. I didn't know what to say to him so I said nothing. I was scared of how he would react but he only saw it as me ignoring him, even though he was only doing the same. He turned to look at me and his eyes narrowed. The look in his eyes was of total hatred, like he didn't want to be anywhere near me.

""What's the matter?" I asked quietly.

"I said leave me alone! I don't want to talk to you!" he replied angrily.

"Okay. I'm sorry. I'll leave you in peace and I'll head up to bed."

And as I stood up he slammed his beer down on the coffee table, looked at me in disgust and shouted,

"FINE! Go to bed. Don't bother trying to put this right. It's your fault I'm in this mood so it's up to you to put it right!"

With that he stood up, marched over to the wishing well he made, well half made, and smashed it to pieces right in front of me. When he finally finished destroying it, he turned around, looked me dead in the eyes and snarled,

"Look what you made me do!"

And as he stared at me in total anger he turned and walked out. He sat in the garden for over an hour and I stayed sat on the sofa, shaking, too scared to even move. Daisy had disappeared upstairs. She was just as terrified as I was and I was sure she would be hiding upstairs somewhere. When Ian eventually came back inside he just sat back down on the sofa.

"I thought you were going to bed?" he snapped.

I was sat on the edge of the sofa and didn't know what to say or do. I knew that he didn't want me there so I stood up, turned to him and said goodnight. He didn't take his eyes off the telly and didn't say a word. I was still shaking in fear. When I got upstairs I found Daisy curled up, hiding in the bath tub. I tried to calm her down and she climbed out and followed me to bed. We snuggled up together all night, comforting each other.

Over the next few days we barely spoke to each other. He would come home from work late at night, sit down with 5 or 6 beers and watch telly till the early hours of the morning. Eventually he would climb into bed and roll away, making it clear he was still mad. The pieces of the well were still all over the living room floor. I couldn't bring myself to look at it yet. It was a really horrible time and I was treading on eggshells all the time. Finally after a week of tension and awkwardness, he was finally in a good mood and we started talking to each other. He was also coming home from work at a good time.

"Shall we watch a film together?" he asked, smiling.

"Yes. I would like that." I replied.

We finally sat down together and actually had a lovely evening. I let Ian choose a film and we cuddled up together with Daisy curled up in front of the fire. By the end of the film Ian was actually smiling again. He looked happy.

"Shall we take Daisy for a nice long walk tomorrow?" he asked.

In my head I couldn't help but be grateful that he was making an effort to spend some time with me.

"Yes that sounds lovely. It's meant to be dry tomorrow as well. We can make a day of it if you like?" I replied, smiling at him.

"Yes that sounds like a good idea to me."

As we cuddled up and watched the film, Ian cracked open a beer and put his arm around me. Finally after what felt like a really long time, I smiled and for a little while I was happy. Out of the corner of my eye I could see Ian was smiling too. We stayed cuddled up for the entire film. The fire was letting out a nice amount of heat and Daisy was really enjoying it. When the film finished it was still early so we decided to watch something else. We were enjoying just sitting with each other. Ian cracked open his 4th beer for that evening as I snuggled back into his arms. I noticed out of the corner of my eye, about half way through the second film, that he was nodding off. I could see his beer tilting more and more. I leaned across, gently took the can from his hand and placed it back on the coffee table. He turned around and moaned but stayed asleep. I stayed and watched the rest of the film. As the film finished, I turned everything off and Daisy and I made our way to bed. I tucked myself into bed and Daisy came and curled up close to me. She definitely wanted some attention now. We cuddled up in bed together, me stroking Daisy as she drifted off to sleep. I lay there for a while, thinking about where we could go for a walk with Daisy the following day. I had a smile on my face for the first time in weeks.

The following morning I woke up and Ian was there next to me.

"Well I'm glad he didn't spend all night on the sofa." I thought to myself.

I went downstairs to let Daisy out in the garden and to make myself a cup of tea. I sat in the living room, drinking my tea, watching the telly, and I wondered what time Ian would get up. Time ticked on by and it was soon 11am, so I decided that I should try and wake him up, so we could get sorted and take Daisy out. I crept upstairs thinking he was still asleep. But he was wide awake on his phone.

"Morning babe." I said, softly.

He turned to look at me and grunted morning back.

"Would you like a cup of tea before we go out?" I asked him.

"Yes please. I'll have it here in bed though, okay." He replied, his eyes fixated on his phone.

Eventually, at about midday he surfaced and he finally got ready to go out. We took Daisy to a nearby woods with a river running through it. She loved it there. Always running all over the place, jumping in the river and back out again. We walked around the woods all afternoon, talking and laughing. Enjoying each others company. It was a wonderful day but I couldn't help but hope that our evening would be too.

Arriving back at home, we both had smiles on our faces and Daisy was actually tired.

"I think that's the first time ever!" Ian exclaimed.

"I think you could be right." I laughed.

It was early evening and we hadn't actually sorted anything out for tea. So we decided to be lazy and order a takeaway. At the same time, we both turned to each other and whispered,

"PIZZA!"

We laughed at each other and ordered from our favourite place. Their pizzas were always amazing. When our food arrived we put on a comedy film and ate together. Unfortunately, I ended up getting a migraine and couldn't stand the light from the telly any more. I needed to lie down in a dark and quiet room.

"I'm sorry baby, but my head is pounding. I'm going to go and lie down in bed for a while and hope it eases soon." I told him softly, holding onto my head.

"Oh, fine! Don't want to spend the evening with me, eh? That's okay, I'll watch the film by myself." he snapped.

"I'm sorry. I'm just really hurting and the lights and noises are making it worse. I just need to lie down in darkness." I explained.

"Fine! Go to bed then!"

I went off to bed and just lay in the dark and quiet for a few hours. After a while, I actually nodded off, but when I did wake up, I was still in pain. Putting my hands on my head, I curled up in a ball under the duvet. I lay there for a while longer and then heard Ian come stumbling up the stairs.

"He must of fallen asleep on the sofa and is still half asleep." I thought to myself.

Ian fell into bed and rolled me over to give me a kiss. I groaned as he did and rolled back over to try and get back to sleep. However, as I did Ian pulled me back around. His hands felt rough on my skin. He pulled me close to him and I groaned again.

"Please can you just let me sleep? My head is still pounding. I don't know what has bought this on." I cried as I pulled the duvet over my head.

Ian tugged at my top, trying to get me to move so he could take it off. But I just moved his hands away from me. He didn't like that though. I could see how annoyed he was getting and how much anger he had inside him.

"Come on babe!" he said, pulling on me again.

"Please!" I begged. That's all I could manage to say.

And as I rolled back around and put my head in my hands Ian sat bolt upright in bed. He gave me a dirty look and got out of bed in a way that I knew he was mad. He picked up the closest thing to him, which happened to be one of his work boots, and threw it across the bedroom. It smashed into the mirror I had on my chest of drawers and broke it, and as it smashed, it startled me. I shot out of bed still clutching onto my head, staring at my broken mirror, confused as to why Ian didn't understand what I was trying to explain to him. He then started shouting at me.

"I can't believe you! Pretending you have a migraine so I'll leave you alone! Saving yourself for your other boyfriend I take it? Such a slag! You really are a bitch!"

I stood there, head pounding and totally speechless. He stormed out of the bedroom and stormed into the spare bedroom. He tucked himself into bed after slamming the door shut. Was he seriously angry with me because I wouldn't sleep with him? I lay in bed, wide awake for hours, my head still pounding. I couldn't stop thinking about what had happened, and I was terrified that this would continue in the morning.

"I've ruined another lovely day!" I thought, punishing myself.

I cried myself to sleep again that night and spent all night tossing and turning. I woke up early the next morning and just sat in bed trying to hear if Ian was awake and up yet. I knew he wouldn't be, he never woke up before me. I was scared to make any sort of noise but Daisy was desperate to go out in the garden, so I snuck downstairs trying not to disturb him. Watching Daisy run around the garden, I listened out for any movement upstairs, but nothing. When Daisy came back inside I sat on the sofa, trying to not make any noise. I didn't even make myself a cup of tea, I just waited until Ian had woken up. However, when he woke up and finally came downstairs he made it apparent that he was still mad. Stomping around upstairs, shouting to himself and slamming doors. Daisy stayed curled up next to me and I put my arm around her to try and keep her calm. As Ian came flying down the stairs and into the living room, Daisy ran past him and upstairs. Ian just looked at me as if to say,

"Now Daisy is upset because of you!"

I knew that look very well. He put his boots on, grabbed his car key and left for work. I knew he was still going to be mad at me but I thought he might of at least said something to me. I didn't know if I should message him or call him to try and apologise, so I just sat for a while, with all sorts going through my head. My head was spinning with so many different things. I spent all day worrying about when Ian would get home, but I knew he would be back late. I got on with some housework and made sure Daisy had a long walk. In the afternoon my mum rang me and we had a long chat, not really about anything in particular. I tried my best to seem like I was happy and not upset. We talked for about an hour and I finally had a smile on my face. I was so close to my mum and she would always make me smile.

As the day wore on it started to get cold, but with Daisy lying across my lap, I was starting to warm up. Although we had a log burner I would never use it myself. Fire was my biggest fear so it was always up to Ian. When Ian did finally come home he marched straight to the kitchen, as per normal, to grab a beer, and then he stormed back into the living room to get the fire lit. As he started to get it going, he looked around the room for some fire wood. Then his eyes fell on the pieces of wishing well. Without a single thought or word, he picked up some of it and threw it on the fire. Once he had sorted the fire out, he sat down on the sofa, put on one of his favourite shows and without even looking a me, he said,

"It will soon be nice and warm in here."

I couldn't believe he did that! He decided to burn the gift he made for me. Really? I didn't know what to say or do. However, I know he had barely said anything to me and had now totally ruined my gift, but he also wasn't screaming or shouting at me. Maybe he had forgotten last night. Whatever it was, I wasn't going to argue about it. He seemed to be in an okay mood. Although I was still upset at the fact that didn't have any respect for me or my things by burning the wishing well, it wasn't worth another night of arguing. I hated the way he would look at me when we argued so it was better for everyone to just go with it. Plus when he shouted and screamed at me I was scared of him. But that was something I would keep to myself.

Over the next few months we continued to have our ups and downs, but mostly we were good. We had been spending time together and we had been talking to each other. We would spend our evenings curled up on the sofa together with Daisy lying in front of the fire. Every so often she would get up and find her favourite toy and throw it across the living room, or we would play with her. She loved it. She loved being curled up by the fire too, but sometimes she would have me worried that she was getting too close.

"Daisy, back!" I would call to her.

As she backed away slowly she would find a cosy place in front of the fire to curl up and sleep. Winter was coming and it was getting much colder, so the fire and the heating were both on more than usual. Which Daisy was happy about.

A couple weeks later my friend, Nadine, who I worked with, invited myself and Ian on a night out with some of her friends in the nearby city. We spent the next few weeks planning and we were both really looking forward to just going out and having a bit of fun. We had been talking about it for weeks. And had everything planned. We decided to have pre drinks at Nadine's, Ian, myself, Nadine and all her other friends. Then we would all head into the city together. Nadine and I were counting down the weeks till our big night out and finally, after all the planning and excitement it was time for our night out. I had my dress out and shoes with it. My dress was a simple, little black dress. As Ian and I got ready we were both in a really good mood so we put on some music. We sang and danced around the bedroom, getting in the party mood. At 7pm we drove over to Nadine's house to meet the rest of her friends and have a few drinks.

I felt like I needed a night to just let my hair down and have fun. And knowing Ian was in such a good mood too, just made everything better. It was the first time in a long time I wasn't worried about us having an argument.

I was really nervous about meeting Nadine's friends, but once we were there and sat with them all it was fine. They were all so lovely, really welcoming. Nadine introduced Ian and I to everyone and we all got talking over some wine. We sat and talked, getting to know everyone, for a few hours. When the taxi bus finally arrived, we all climbed in, giggling with one another and made our way to the city for our big night out. About 40 minutes later we arrived at a busy bar and we all jumped out. The guys walking ahead and all the girls walking behind. Holding the doors open, Ian winked at me and I smiled to myself. We all stood at the bar deciding what to drink and then we all found a table for us to sit around, talking and laughing. The night was off to a great start and we were all getting on great. After about an hour we moved on to the next bar. The next bar was even better then the first and they did so many cocktails. We all tried 3 different ones each, and we all loved them. My favourite had skittles in it! I was starting to get a bit worried about Ian, he was drinking a lot and very quickly. But it was no different to any other night, so I tried not to overthink it. We stayed in that bar for quite a while and had a lovely time. But then it was soon time to head off to the nearby club. When we arrived it was still closed so we had a drink in pub next door while we waited. It was a lovely evening so we decided to sit outside. Ian and I sat next to each other, but for some reason, as Ian sat down he moved his chair away from me. I didn't think much of it and we all sat and chatted for a while. Ian was starting to get quite loud and boisterous, and I could tell he was getting quite drunk. He was laughing and smiling though, and that made me happy. All of a sudden a couple of girls came over to us and began talking to us. I thought Nadine knew them at first, but then she looked at me with a very confused look on her face, and all her friends looked at us both in the same way. They were both quite drunk and falling all over the place.

"I'm Tiffany, and this is Sara!" one of them slurred at one of the boys, Jason.

Jason brushed them off and looked at his partner, grabbing her hand. Tiffany and Sara looked around the table at all of us, slurring their words and not making much sense. They were harmless enough and we all giggled at the way they were talking to us. I got up to go to the toilet and Nadine came with me.

"I'm having such a great time. Thank you so much for inviting us both out." I exclaimed.

"It's been such a good night so far. Thank you for coming." Nadine replied.

As we wondered back outside to our table we both stopped in out tracks when we spotted Tiffany and Sara sitting on Ian's lap. The three of them were giggling and flirting with each other. Ian noticed that we were back but didn't even give me a second look. Nadine and I looked at each other, and all her friends looked up at me too. One of the guys, Aaron, looked me dead in the eyes and whispered,

"I'm so sorry. We did try!"

I turned to look at Ian again and walk over to him and make some sort of conversation. He still couldn't even look at me. He was too busy flirting. I was so angry with him and

I could tell everyone else was starting to get annoyed with him too. I wondered over to him to sit back down next to him and both Tiffany and Sara gave me a dirty look. The club was about to open so I turned to Ian and said quietly,

"Look, the club is about to open, shall we go and get in the queue?"

Everyone else mumbled that we should, so they all finished their drinks and gathered their things. I picked up my jacket and handbag and stood in front of Ian. We were all stood waiting on him. Nobody knew if they should say or do anything so they just whispered to themselves behind me. I was so mad and embarrassed but I didn't want to have an argument in front of everyone. I didn't know what to say or do. All I knew was that I wanted to go home. Eventually, Tiffany and Sara got off of Ian's lap and he said goodbye to them. I saw the look in his eyes, I hadn't seen it in months. His eyes lit up and there was a sparkle there. The way he used to look at me. He now looked at skinny, big boobed, blonde haired girls with that same spark, but never at me. Not for months.

Getting up off his chair he grabbed his jacket and turned towards the club, still not saying a word.

"Amanda, honey. What he just did in front of you and us, was totally inappropriate. You need to talk to him about it." Nadine expressed.

"I know. I will have a chat with him about it." I replied.

I was shocked that everyone seemed to be on my side. Ian had always made it clear to me that everything was my fault and I was always in the wrong. But as much as I said I would talk to him about it, I was absolutely terrified of how he would react and what he would say. We all joined him in the queue, everyone chatting away and giggling. Ian and I stood side by side, not talking at the time. Eventually, I plucked up the courage to say something.

"What was all the flirting with those two girls about?" I asked, quietly.

"What? Flirting with them? How ridiculous do you sound? I wasn't flirting with them!" he laughed.

"Of course you were. They were both sat on your lap. Laughing and joking and all over each other, and completely ignoring me in the process."

As mad as I was, I stayed calm and didn't shout or get angry with him. I just knew I had to say something.

He turned to look at me and then looked behind us at everyone else. Then back round to the front of the queue.

"I WAS NOT FUCKING FLIRTING!" he yelled, and just as he did the bouncers started letting us in.

I stood in shock for a second, and everyone behind us just stared at me. I turned to look at them and made excuses for him. Things like 'he was annoyed because we were stood waiting' and 'don't worry, let me go and calm him down.' However, I could tell they all didn't know what to say or do, but they all let me deal with Ian the way I said I would. So I followed him inside the club and as we got inside, I pulled him to one side as the others walked past us, knowing we would catch them up. He gave me that look of hatred that I was so used to, which made my heart pound so much harder and faster than normal. As I pulled him to one side I was so focused on talking to him I didn't realise there was a bar right there. He stood with his back to me and ordered himself a rum and coke, not acknowledging that I was next to him. He then went to sit at a nearby table so I followed him and sat next to him.

"Look, I don't want to fall out and argue about it, we are having a good night. But the three of you were all over each other and it made me feel really uncomfortable" I shouted over the music, trying to explain how I felt.

"Will you just leave me alone! I wasn't flirting and neither were they! We were just talking and laughing. You have ruined tonight by saying something so stupid!" he yelled.

"I'm sorry, but that is how it looked! They were sat on your lap!" I replied.

"Well no one else thinks that! See, they all thought you were overreacting. Like you always do, and they have left you."

From the moment we sat down he couldn't look at me but those kind of comments kept coming. No matter how much I tried to tell him what he had done was wrong, the more he twisted it to being my fault. I started to get really upset and started crying in the club. I was so embarrassed. I had no idea how long we had been sat there but Ian's comments got meaner the more he drank, as per normal. I was so hurt, upset and embarrassed that I had to walk away. As I stood up, I dried my eyes and wondered off to find Nadine and everyone else. I wondered round the club for ages, but I couldn't find anyone. In the end I pulled my phone out of my handbag and found my way to the toilet to call Nadine.

"NADINE! Where are you?" I sobbed.

"Oh my god! Amanda! What's that matter?" she asked.

"All we have done since getting in the club is argue. He's had too much to drink! Where are you?" I replied.

"We thought you had both left as we couldn't find you. We are on the way home now. I'm so sorry!"

With tears rolling down my cheeks, I realised I was now alone with him, drunk and in the city. I felt so alone. After pulling myself together, I made my way back to Ian. He was still sat in the same place with 4 empty glasses. I sat down opposite him and shouted to him over the music.

"Nadine and everyone else have gone home. What do you want to do?"

Without saying a word, he stood up and started stumbling towards the exit. I stood up quickly, grabbing my bag and jacket, rushing after him.

"I guess he wants to go home." I thought to myself.

I followed him outside and we started looking for a taxi home. Ian still wasn't saying anything to me. I tried saying plenty, but he was totally ignoring me. Then all of a sudden he shouted at the top of his voice, whilst slurring and falling over himself,

"FUCK OFF! I'M GOING HOME ALONE! FIND YOUR OWN WAY BACK! GO AWAY!"

I stopped in my tracks as he continued to find a taxi. I started to panic. If he left me I would have no way of getting home. He had all the money and I didn't know the city. I knew that him going home alone wasn't an option so I made sure I was close to him. Eventually, we found a taxi, both climbed in and began the 40 minute car ride home. I was glad we were finally making our way home and that he now wouldn't shout at me because of the taxi driver being there. About half way home Ian fell asleep and I let out a sigh of relief. I knew that when we got home he would fall asleep as soon as he sat down. Arriving home, I unlocked the front door and Ian fell through it and stumbled over to the sofa. He slumped down and glanced at the coffee table and noticed an unopened can of beer. He cracked it open and I sat down next to him. I had hoped that he would practically fall straight to sleep. I was so glad we had taken Daisy to Ian's parents for the night.

"I don't want you near me after you ruined tonight!" he slurred.

"Well, I would like to make this right, but I think right now we both need to get to bed and try to get some sleep. It's been a long night." I suggested, thinking he needed to sleep if off rather than keep drinking.

"I want to be alone! Go to bed by yourself!" he shouted.

He turned his head back towards the telly and grabbed the remote. I watched as he put a random programme on that he wasn't even going to watch. Once he had chosen, he curled up in the corner of the sofa. Because he wasn't watching, I turned the volume down and then made my way up to bed. I tiptoed up to bed, alone and upset. He must of fallen asleep straight away as there was no movement and the volume didn't go back up again. I lay in bed for hours thinking about everything that happened that night. Then my phone pinged,

"Hi Amanda, I really hope you're okay and managed to get everything sorted and get home okay. You know where I am if you need me. Love Nadine." the text read.

As I lay there in bed by myself and read the message, a tear rolled down my face. I cried myself to sleep again and spent all night tossing and turning. So much was running through my mind. Soon, morning came and when I woke up, Ian was there next to me, still fast asleep. I knew he would sleep for a couple more hours yet, so I made my way downstairs and made myself a cup of tea. I was dreading him waking up and the shouting and arguing starting again. But I tried to think of something else and I started to message Nadine. We spent most of the morning messaging each other and it took my mind off the issues with Ian. Ian and I didn't have any plans for that particular Sunday apart from picking up Daisy and taking her a for walk, so I left him to sleep and wake up in his own time. And as much as the previous night was a nightmare, our 1 year anniversary was only a couple of weeks away. So I decided to start having a look at what we could do and where we could go. When Ian finally woke up and came downstairs he seemed to be in a really good mood, even with a hangover.

"What time did we get home last night? I don't remember getting back, to be honest I don't really remember much." he laughed, quietly.

"I didn't actually look at what time we got back, I just know it was early hours. How are you feeling?" I asked nervously.

"Apart from a pounding headache, I feel fine. From what I do remember, it was a good night. Would you like another cuppa?" he asked.

"Yes, please." I replied, a little surprised. He never offered to make me a drink.

We spent the rest of the morning just relaxing and after lunch we left to go and pick up Daisy and then we took her the local woods. We had a lovely afternoon strolling through the woods and when we got home we cuddled up on the sofa with a film on. We had had a lovely day and I was actually happy. I could see Ian was happy too.

About a week later I was starting to really think about our one year anniversary. One evening sat together, actually eating tea together for the first time in a long time so I thought I would talk to him about it.

"Guess what is next week?" I exclaimed.

"I don't know." He replied with a mouthful of food.

"It's our one year anniversary. Can you believe we have been together a year? I thought we could go out and do something together. What do you think?" I asked, excitedly.

"Hmm? Oh, yeah sure we can do something. I promise I'll sort something out for one evening next week." He said, unconvincingly, but I still believed him.

Later that evening I was messaging Nadine, telling her what Ian had promised me. I was so excited. I couldn't help but wonder what we might do, where we might go. Just to spend some time as the two of us would be really great. I was so excited.

I spent the following week wondering, counting down and excited about it. I had also bought him a little gift of a rustic looking photo frame with his favourite picture in it and a voucher for an afternoon tea for the two of us at an amazing looking hotel. Ian hadn't mentioned it again in the week before but I just thought he was planning something. We would both be working during the day but we would have the evening together, and I was looking forward to spending that time together. However, two days before, I spoke to him in the evening about it, so I had some sort of idea, and I'm not great at surprises so I was sneakily trying to find out our plan. But he completely shattered the promises had made to me.

"So, can I have a little clue about what we might be doing for our anniversary? You know, where we are going or even if we are going out or staying in?" I giggled, excitedly.

He turned to look at me, confusion across his face.

"What do you mean 'doing for our anniversary?' We will both be at work all day and I could be late home as the boys are talking about going to the pub that evening. So we won't be doing anything." He said, making it clear he was annoyed that I even suggested doing something.

"But you promised me we would do something together for our anniversary in the evening. Please baby. You could maybe suggest going to the pub the following night?" I suggested.

"Well firstly, I never promised you anything and secondly the boys won't change the night. Plus I'll be working late the rest of this week. So no, we won't be doing anything. Just leave it at that, okay!" he huffed at me, as he stormed off to the kitchen to grab another beer.

I couldn't believe it. I remember the conversation we had and he definitely promised me. I knew he did.

"You did promise me we could do something. Even if we just had a nice meal here and go out for a couple of drinks after." I tried explaining.

"I did NOT say any such thing! Get it in your thick head, we are NOT doing anything. End of conversation! Retard!" he shouted, as he stormed outside.

I was so upset. I had been looking forward to giving him his gifts and us spending the evening looking back at all our good memories over the past year. But it now looked like we weren't going to anything all week. And I really didn't know what to do with his gifts.

"I am sure he promised?" I thought to myself, confused.

He seemed to be so adamant about not promising, so maybe I was imagining it, or I was going crazy but I decided to leave it so the shouting didn't get any worse. I left him to sit outside to calm down for a while, and when he eventually came back inside, I decided to say goodnight and head up to bed. He had calmed down enough to mumble goodnight back, but not enough for a kiss and cuddle so I left him to watch his programme. Daisy followed me to bed and we both fell asleep cuddled up together.

Two days later it was our anniversary and I wasn't expecting anything. I was hoping he would at least say something. But nothing at all from him all day. I didn't see him in the morning so I sent him a message later on that read,

"Happy anniversary baby! 1 year already. I can't wait to make more amazing memories! Have a good day and I'll speak to you later. Love you xxxx"

As I pressed send, I smiled. One whole year. I couldn't believe it. I was still a little upset because we couldn't do anything to celebrate. I waited and waited for him to reply, but he never did. Hours passed and I was starting to worry. I knew was busy, but if I had messaged him by now he would usually reply. Sometimes anyway. I didn't hear anything from him all day and by 7'o'clock in the evening I figured he must be at the pub. So I decided to try calling him just to make sure he was okay. As I pressed the call button on my phone my head was in my throat and pounding really fast. He would always get cross with me for calling him at any time of the day, but because I hadn't heard from him and I was worried, I just wanted to make sure he was okay. As the phone rang I thought about hanging up and just waiting, but then he answered,

"What? I'm with the boys! What do you want?" he blurted down the phone.

"I just wanted to make sure you were okay. Did you get my message earlier?" I asked him.

"Yes, I did. Now can you leave me alone to have a good night with the lads? He snapped.

"Oh, um okay. Well have a good time and I'll see..."

Before I could even finish what I was saying, he cut me off. I sat back down on the sofa, Daisy looking at me from the floor.

"Come on, Daisy." I said, patting the cushion next to be.

Daisy joined me on the sofa and we sat together for the rest of the evening. I didn't hear anything else from Ian all night. I sat and cuddled Daisy and watched a film when suddenly my phone pinged. I had hoped it would be Ian, but it was an invitation. As I read through the message I realised that it was for a 10 year school reunion. It was a group message and everyone was invited and plans were being made. I was in two minds as to whether to go or not. I hadn't spoken to any of them for years, but after talking in the group chat for a while, I decided that I wanted to go. I was actually looking forward to seeing everyone. We all started to make plans for in a months time to give everyone time to respond and to find a venue. Because of arranging the reunion I started to talk to a few people I was friends with at school and it was great to reminisce and catch up with them. By the end of the evening I was smiling and looking forward to it.

"When a date is set I will sit down with Ian and tell him about it." I told myself.

By about half past ten I started to feel a bit tired and I could see Daisy was ready for bed, so we made our way up to bed. Ian still hadn't messaged and I had absolutely no idea when he would be home. But I tucked myself up into bed and slowly drifted off to sleep with Daisy by my side. At about 3 in the morning I heard the door open and slam shut. He was finally home. I heard him stumbling around downstairs and then silence. I lay there, listening, but nothing. I snuck downstairs to make sure he was okay. He was sprawled out on the sofa, fast asleep. I breathed a sigh of relief and then made my way back up to bed.

Over the next week a date for the reunion had been set, so I sat Ian down to tell him about it. I was nervous to tell him but excited about seeing old friends again.

"Ian, baby. Some people I went to school with have organised a 10 year reunion in a couple of weeks time. I'm thinking about showing my face." I told him.

"A 10 year reunion? What for? Are partners going?" he replied.

"Yes. I think there are a few people that want to get everyone together. I think I might go. As for partners going, I don't know. No one has said anything but I will find out." I explained.

"Well, I think it's weird but we will see closer to the time."

As he said that my jaw hit the floor. Why were we going to wait and see? I didn't know what he meant but I could hear the frustration in his voice, so I changed the subject.

"Shall we take Daisy up to the field for a run around?"

"I'll take her in a minute!" he snapped.

He was definitely annoyed with me, again. So I just left him to it, I didn't push for anything. I just sat next to him and watched the telly with him. After 20 minutes, Ian took Daisy outside and walked up to the field for about 45 minutes. When he did eventually get back the 3 of us made our way to bed.

"Yet again he is annoyed with me. Was it really just because I mentioned the reunion?" I thought to myself as I lay in bed, wide awake.

Over the next few days I found out more and more about the reunion and I had been told that partners weren't invited. As I found out more about it, the more I was actually looking forward to it. I told Ian that the venue had been chosen and booked and that partners weren't invited. He really didn't like that though.

"What? No partners? Well then you're not going!" he boomed.

I was so shocked. My smile turned into a frown almost instantly. I didn't know what to say.

"What do you mean not going? I've been looking forward to it and all of my school friends are going to be there. I've said I'm going." I explained, trying to stand up for myself.

I didn't understand why he was getting so mad and saying I couldn't go. I sat there for a minute, waiting for his response. Eventually, he turned to look at me and he had a smirk across his face, as if to say 'you will do as I say.'

"If partners aren't invited, then you're not going. Who knows what you will do and what will happen."

"I would of liked it if partners were invited, but it's just a few drinks with some people I went to school with. I promise you that's all it will be, just a catch up. I'll stay at mum and dad's for the night and then will be back lunchtime the following day. I can promise you, hand on heart, nothing bad will happen." I said, softly.

He gave me a dirty look and shook his head at me. I decided to leave it at that as I didn't want it to turn into a massive argument. I knew he was waiting for a bigger reaction to what he said, but I left him to think about what I had said. We spent the rest of the evening not really speaking to each other, each time I tried to say something he just mumbled back at me, still fixated on the telly. As it got later and later I was getting more and more tired, and I could see Daisy was tired too.

"I'm going to head up to bed now. Goodnight baby." I said softly as I leaned in to give him a kiss.

He didn't move his head at all so I just kissed him on the cheek and stood up. As I stood up, Daisy stirred and realised where I was going so she got up and followed me to bed.

"Goodnight." Ian grumbled as I left the living room.

As I climbed into bed, Daisy jumped up onto the bed with me. She snuggled up close and I smiled. She always put a smile on my face. Having Daisy with me always calmed me down and with her close by made me happy. So falling asleep with her next to me was perfect and I fell asleep smiling for the first time in a while. I don't know what time Ian climbed into bed, but when he did he woke me up. He flopped into bed like a dead weight, and as soon as he did I could feel his cold, hard hands on my body. I was still half asleep and pushed his hands off of me. But he put them back. This continued a few times. I could feel him getting angry.

"Come on!" he whispered, whilst kissing my back.

"Cant he just leave me alone? If I pretend to be asleep, he should leave me alone!" I thought to myself.

But he didn't stop. His hands were all over my body and they felt like sand paper. As they ran over me I tensed. Praying he would stop. As he got on top of me I told him to stop as I was still half asleep, but as I said it I remembered how he acted last time I said no. All of a sudden I felt like I had to, just to stop any arguing or shouting. And because I felt like I had to, I let it happen. And that's how it was for the rest of our relationship. Anything to stop him shouting at me, calling me names and throwing things. I buried my feelings deep down, and he never knew how I felt but honestly, he wouldn't of cared anyway.

Over the next couple of weeks we would have some smaller arguments but generally things were good between us. Ian was still working a lot and we didn't do much in the evenings but we spent Sundays together. He seemed to be happy. However, the reunion was a matter of days away, and I knew I had to talk to him about it again. But I was adamant that I was going to go. I hadn't spoken to my parents about it either but I knew they would be okay with me staying over for the night. A few days before I plucked up the courage to speak to Ian.

"Ian baby, can I have a word please?" I asked.

"Yeah, no problem. Let me just grab a drink." he replied, and off he went to grab his first beer of the evening.

He sat down next to me on the sofa and right at that moment I could see he was in a good mood. I thought twice about talking to him about it, even considered not going. But then I had a sudden wave of bravery and I just blurted it out.

"My school reunion is on Saturday evening so I'll be staying at mum and dad's that night. But like I said before, I promise nothing bad will happen. Please don't be mad but I do want to go." I explained to him.

"I have already said you're not going!" he snapped at me.

"These are people I went to school with and it's for one night. But it's okay for you to go out with your friends. I have told them that I will be there and have plans sorted." I was starting to get annoyed now.

We ended up arguing about it but I wasn't backing down. When he realised that, he said he had one condition.

"You message me all night and call me a few times throughout the night!" he ordered.

"Fine. No problem. But I won't be bombarding you with messages if you're not replying." I agreed.

So, I was going but I had to make sure we were talking all night. But if he didn't reply I wasn't just going to message him all night with no reply. I agreed to talk to him throughout the night. Texts and calls. With Ian finally agreeing that I could go, I spoke to my parents about it and they were both looking forward to seeing me, even if it was only for a short while. On Saturday morning Ian left for work and

I got everything ready to take with me for that evening. I planned on leaving just after lunch so I could have tea with my parents and then get ready to head out. I was getting so nervous about seeing everyone and wondered who would actually be there. I was about ready to leave for my parents house, so I called Ian to let him know, and to make sure he was okay.

"I'm really busy. What do you want?" he snapped.

"I just wanted to make sure you're okay and just let you know I'm off to mum and dad's. I'll let you know I'm there okay." I replied.

"Okay. Speak to you later." he said quickly, and with that he hung up the phone.

So I got in the car and drove to my parents. I was so excited to see them. Half an hour later I arrived and I rushed through the door to see them. There were big cuddles as soon as I walked through the door. We sat and talked for hours before we sat together at the table for our tea and had so many laughs. I had missed them so much. We talked and laughed until I went to get ready for the evening. I listened to some music whilst getting ready and had a couple glasses of wine. I was in such a good mood and singing along to the music, smiling. However, I was starting to get really anxious about seeing everyone again though. But I just kept thinking that everything would be okay.

"I know a few of the people definitely going!" I smiled, trying to calm myself down.

Since I had messaged Ian to let him know I had arrived, I hadn't heard anything from him, but I would message again a bit later on when I had arrived at the social club. So when I did finally get there and start talking to a couple of old friends, I got a drink and messaged him.

"Hey baby. Just got here and I'm with an old friend. She was one of my closest friends at school and it's so nice to see her. How has your day been? You going to do much this evening?"

As I pressed send, I wondered when I would hear back from him. I put my phone back in my bag and carried on talking, checking my phone constantly. Each time I checked, nothing. So I carried on with the night. It was a really good night but I hadn't heard anything from Ian all night. The following day I messaged him to say that I would be home in a few hours. But I still didn't hear anything back from him. I was starting to worry, so after about an hour I decided to call him. I knew he would be awake by then. He would have to be with Daisy.

"What?" he grumbled.

"I just wanted to make sure you're okay. I didn't hear from you all last night or this morning." I replied.

"You never messaged me last night! That was the deal we had. And nothing!" he snarled.

"I did message you when I got there. I never heard back from you. I kept checking my phone all night to see if you had replied, but nothing."

He started shouting all sorts down the phone at me and I was starting to get really upset.

"Look, I don't want to have an argument over the phone about this. I will be home in an hour or two and we can talk about it then." I said, calmly, but dreading getting home.

"Fine, we will have this out when you get home. But get back soon!" he replied, and then hung up the phone.

I stayed for a little while longer, but I was so worried about getting home. I kept looking at the clock to check the time. I knew we were going to have an argument when I got home and no matter how much I wanted to stay longer, it would only make it worse. So after about 15 minutes, I said my goodbyes and made my way home. My heart was in my throat the whole way home, knowing it wasn't going to be an enjoyable evening. When I did arrive home, Ian and I sat down to discuss the previous night practically as soon as I walked in. The shouting started almost instantly. He didn't ask me anything about my evening at all, just shouted at me. We argued all evening about me not messaging him. I told him that I had sent two message and that I never heard back from him. I even explained that I would even show him the messages on my phone. But he wasn't interested. I tried my hardest to explain it all to him, but he just wouldn't listen to me, as per usual.

"I never had any messages from you all night!" he shouted.

I spent the whole evening crying and apologising . He called me all sorts of names and didn't believe I had stayed at my parents. I did everything I could to make him believe me. After arguing for an hour he stormed outside and stayed out there for about an hour. When he came back inside, I tried to make things right and apologised one more time. But, all of a sudden, he picked up my empty mug off of the coffee table and threw it as hard as he could across the whole length of the living room, scaring me stiff in the process. He marched upstairs to the bathroom and then I heard a loud thud. I jumped in my seat, again with my heart in my throat and instantly knew that something was broken which turned out to be the door of the cupboard under the bathroom sink. Looking across the room with tears in my eyes, I noticed tea all across the walls so I began to clean it off. Poor Daisy had hidden herself in the corner of the living room. Ian stormed back downstairs and sat back on the sofa, giving me a dirty look, as he always did. I didn't say anything and neither did he, Daisy ran upstairs to hide away from it all. Ian sat there, drinking beer after beer, just watching the telly, and I just sat there not knowing what to say. Eventually I noticed Ian had nodded off, so I gently took the can out of his hand so it didn't spill, turned the telly off and made my way up to bed. As I walked past the bathroom I heard Daisy jump out of the bath and scratch at the door to be let out.

"Aw, poor Daisy!" I thought to myself, opening the door for her.

As she ran out, I caught a glimpse of the cupboard door an my heart sank. He had kicked the door in and it was completely smashed and I was devastated at the sight of it. I knew it would have to be sorted sooner rather than later, but I also knew that it would take Ian months to get it fixed. I would have to talk to him about it in the morning. I climbed into bed with Daisy beside me and as I stroked her gently, we both drifted off to sleep.

The following weeks and months were very up and down. But when we were good, we were both really happy, and I kept telling myself that. One afternoon while Ian was at work, my mum called me with an idea.

"How do you feel about an activity holiday? All six of us. Me, your dad, you, Ian, your sister Tessa and her partner Sam? Your dad and I are thinking five days at an activity based holiday site later this year." she started explaining.

"Oh, wow! That sounds like great fun. Yeah I'm definitely up for that. I'll have a word with Ian tonight. What kind of activities are there?" I asked.

We talked on the phone about it for ages and I was already so excited. Mum sent me an email with a list of all the activities on it and all sorts of other information.

"I haven't spoken to Tessa yet but I'm going to speak to her about it when she finishes work. I'll let you know what she says, and you let me know what Ian says and then we can look into getting it booked." Mum explained.

"Yes okay. I'll look through the activities too and see what takes my fancy." I replied, excitedly.

As we said our goodbyes, I was giddy with excitement. I couldn't wait to start planning, and I couldn't wait to speak to Ian that evening. I spent the rest of the afternoon looking through the information and the activities and made a list of what I would like to do. When Ian finally came home he could tell that I was in a good mood.

"Why are you so happy?" he asked as he walked through the door.

"Well, I've got something exciting to talk to you about. I'll let you get in first and then we can talk about it." I said with a big smile on my face.

He huffed and walked straight to the kitchen. He got himself a beer and then got settled on the sofa after saying hello to Daisy, then I began to explain.

"Mum rang me earlier, how do you feel about an activity holiday later this year, all six of us? Mum has sent me some information and the list of activities so I can show you that now. I think it will be great fun." I told him, excitedly.

The look he gave me was one I hadn't seen before. Almost disgust and confusion together. He sat there for a second before saying anything, but eventually said,

"Holiday? With your family? What kind of activities are there?" he asked.

"I have the list here. Have a look and let me know what you want to do. Then I can let mum know and go from there." I replied, handing him my phone.

As he scrolled through the list, I waited for him to start telling me the activities that he would want to do, but he didn't say anything. Once he had finished reading through, he turned to me and looked at me as if I was crazy.

"There is nothing here that I would want to do." He snapped, throwing my phone back at me.

"Well, have a think and you might decide on something. I have started to make a list on what I like the sound of. Then we can get planning with everyone." I said, smiling.

He just looked at me and shrugged his shoulders. I wasn't convinced he even wanted to go, and then I suddenly started to worry that he would try and stop me from going. Over the following weeks my mum and I talked a lot about it and I was talking to my sister a lot about it too. We were all really excited but there was one problem. Ian wasn't giving me any sort of answer and I was getting frustrated with him. So one evening I sat him down and said we really needed to discuss this family holiday.

"Ugh. Do we have to?" he asked, showing absolutely no interest at all.

"We really need to sort out what activities we want to do. See what we agree on with everyone else. This is the list

I have made for a what I like the sound of." I explained, as I passed him my list.

He took the list from my hand and glanced down at it. I was sat on the edge of the sofa, excited to sort it all out and then he turned to me and looked at me as if I was stupid.

"Why do you think I would want to do any of these? None of them interest me at all. And honestly I don't think we should even go!" he snarled.

My smile disappeared instantly and my heart sank. I could feel a lump starting to form in my throat. I couldn't let him stop me from going, but I didn't know what to say. We both just sat there for a second, waiting for the other to say something. Eventually, I plucked up the courage to say something.

"It's a family holiday, you don't have to go if you really don't want to but I still want to go. We haven't been able to go on holiday as a family for years so I would love to go with them." I explained, trying to hold back the tears.

"Well, I'm definitely not going and I don't really want you to go either!" he ordered, throwing the piece of paper back at me.

"What? Why? They are my family and I really would love to go." I cried.

He then proceeded to guilt me more than he ever had before. He told me that he would spend the five days so worried about me, and find it so hard with me not being around that he wouldn't eat or sleep for the whole time I was away. I told him that I would think about it but I knew I had to find a way of going. My family and I had already started planning and had booked some activities. We were all really excited, but I still needed to figure out what Ian was going to do and make sure he understood that I was definitely going.

It was now only a month before the holiday and I was so worried about telling him and leaving him alone. But I knew I had to tell him.

"Ian, babe. My family holiday is in a months time. I just wanted to remind you that I'll be leaving early on the Monday and back late on the Friday." I told him.

As an argument started, I tried and tried to get him to understand. I told him that I had paid for everything and that it was all organised. I couldn't let him stop me from spending time with my family. He stopped me enough of the time when I just want to spend a day with them. Eventually, he began to back down a little, but he continued to make me feel as guilty as he possibly could.

"Fine! Go! But just know when I don't eat or sleep properly that week, it's YOUR fault! And you message and call me all the time. Then I might believe that you won't run off with anyone else!" he barked at me as he stormed outside.

I sat there with tears rolling down my cheeks, relieved that I could actually go, but also already dreading coming home and the argument that would inevitably happen. He sat outside for a long time and I stayed sat on the sofa.

"A month." I thought to myself. "A month and I can have a bit of time away from him."

Within that month Ian became quite clingy. At the time it made me happy, he was showing me affection so I thought things were changing for the better. He started talking about marriage and babies for us one day. And then one day he turned to me and said,

"I think I am ready to a baby!" he exclaimed, with a huge grin on his face.

I went into complete panic. I was certainly not ready to have a baby with him. I didn't know what to say so I nervously giggled and carried on cooking our tea. He kept mentioning it all evening, so in the end I had to just be as honest as I could be without causing an argument.

"I don't think we are really in a place to be ready right now. And we have only been together 18 months."

As the words came out of my mouth I saw the frustration in his eyes but nothing more was said about it, so I carried on tidying the kitchen. The next day, I was cooking our tea again and we sat down together to eat. We sat and talked about our days and when we finished I cleared everything away and went to pick up my contraceptive tablet, but it wasn't in its normal place. I searched all over the kitchen for them but they were nowhere to be seen.

"Ian, have you seen my contraceptive tablets?" I asked, curiously.

"No! Not at all." He replied, calmly. Very calmly for him in fact.

I carried on searching, and nothing. Luckily, I had the next strip of tablets that I could use instead and I said nothing else about it. In fact, a couple days later I had completely forgotten all about it.

All of a sudden it was the weekend before my family holiday and I was running around making sure I had everything ready to be packed. Ian spent most of the weekend moping around, still trying to make me feel guilty for going. On the Sunday evening we had planned to sit together and watch a film, but I decided to go for a shower first. Standing in the shower, with the hot water rolling over my skin, I couldn't help but smile. Proper time with my family for five whole days. I was ready to go and my bag was packed. I turned the water off and pulled back the curtain and out of the corner of my eye, I saw something on top of the cupboard above the sink. I wrapped myself in the towel and reached across. It felt like a... pill packet? Surely not?

"What on earth?" I thought to myself.

I looked at the packet in disbelief. It was my missing tablet strip.

"How did they get there? And how have I not seen them before now?" I asked myself.

And then it hit me. The conversations Ian and I had had in the previous week's and his disappointment when I said I wasn't ready for a baby right now. My jaw dropped as I figured out that Ian must of tried to hide them there to try and stop me from taking the tablets. I was in shock and so angry. How could he do something like that? I knew I had to confront him, but how was I going to do that without causing a huge argument the night before I was to leave for a week. I went back downstairs, tablets in my hand ready to confront him.

"Look what I found upstairs. My tablets. Do you know how they got in the bathroom?" I asked him.

"No, how would I know how they got there? They are your tablets. What exactly are you accusing me of?"

"Well, I'm just asking if you put them on top of the cupboard above the sink? I didn't put them there and you're the only other person in the house. I'm just asking if you moved them there."

The look of absolute disgust on his face. As if to say 'how could you say something like that?' I knew by the look on his face that he was just going to deny it, but I could tell he was lying. Anyway, it had to be him that moved them. As the argument got worse and the shouting got louder, I started to doubt myself and what I thought to be true. I started to think I was going crazy for even thinking he might move them. Was I going crazy? Did I move them myself? By the end of the evening he had convinced me that there was no way that he would ever of hidden them from me. So much so that I had apologised to him. The evening had run away from us because we had argued so much, so we both sat with Daisy for a little while before heading to bed. After about 20 minutes I could hear Ian snoring very lightly, so I turned the telly off and moved his beer can and made my way to bed. Still questioning myself from the earlier argument. But as I entered the bedroom I saw my suitcase and I started smiling. In a matter of hours I would be on my way to spend an amazing holiday with my family. I fell asleep with a smile on my face. My alarm was set for 7:30 so I could finish packing and make sure I had everything I needed. When my alarm went off in the morning I jumped out of bed, trying not to disturb Ian. I finished packing and made sure I was ready to go. Now I was just waiting to be picked up by my parents, but turns out I still had quite a while to wait for them. I decided to take Daisy for a quick run while Ian was still sleeping. I knew he wouldn't actually get out of bed until after I had left, so I left him sleep until I knew my parents were 10 minutes away. I stood and watched as Daisy ran around the field and chuckled to myself as she bounced up and down in the long grass. I wasn't out with her for too long, I knew she would get a proper walk later on, and after 20 minutes we made our way back home and as we walked through the door, my phone pinged.

"We are about 10 minutes away honey. Make sure you are outside ready so we can head straight off." the message read.

I grinned and looked down at Daisy.

"I'm going to miss you my beautiful girly. You make sure you be good." I told her as I knelt down to give her a cuddle.

I sat with her for a moment, enjoying just being with her, my best friend. Suddenly realising my bags were still upstairs, I stood up to get them and say goodbye to Ian. I hoped it would just be a case of saying goodbye with no shouting or guilt trip. Luckily, he was still so tired he just said goodbye, gave me a hug and rolled over. He mumbled that he would call in a while but I MUST call when we got there and throughout the week. I agreed, kissed him on the cheek, grabbed my bags and made my way downstairs. By the time I had put my shoes on my parents had just pulled up. I said goodbye to Daisy again and left, thankful for this week away from Ian, but I was going to worry about the pair of them. The thought of staying did cross my mind, again, but I brushed myself off and made my way outside. Both my mum and dad jumped out of the car and gave me a big hug.

"This is going to be an amazing week!" my mum squealed.

And as we all climbed into the car I felt like I was home, and I couldn't wait to see my sister. The drive would take about 3 hours and we were meeting Tessa and Sam there. The 3 hours in the car flew by so quickly and we arrived there first. We made a start emptying the car and having a look around the apartment. About ten minutes later Tessa and Sam arrived and we all went running up to each other and all hugged each other tightly. We helped them bring everything inside and then we all got settled. We had so much planned for the next few days and it was going to be so much fun. As time went on it was getting close to tea time so as mum started cooking, Tessa and I sat and had a catch up.

"Oh, Mandy I have missed you so much! I have been counting down the weeks and days for this!" Tessa exclaimed, as she gave me another big hug.

We sat together until tea was ready, laughing like we always would. Suddenly, I realised that I hadn't messaged Ian to let him know that we arrived safely, so I grabbed my phone and let him know. In all the excitement it had slipped my mind. I had half expected a message from him, but nothing. Then I noticed that the signal on my phone was awful. I started to panic a bit but managed to make sure nobody noticed and just tried to find some signal to send a message. Eventually, I managed to get the message sent so I put my phone back in my pocket and sat down at the table. The whole family around the table again. It was amazing. After eating we cleared up and then it was time for our first activity. Badminton. So we made our way to the badminton courts. When we arrived we were the only ones there. There were about eight courts and they were all empyt. So we spread out and played for about an hour and a half. All of us running around, puffing and panting and all rosy cheeked. We all had such a great time and once we were all totally worn out we made our way back to our apartment to play games. We somehow managed to get lost on our way back in the dark. We all found it hilarious. A walk that should of taken 10 minutes, took us 40. None of us knew how we managed it, but we really didn't care and couldn't stop laughing. When we did finally make it back, we all poured ourselves a drink and sat back around the table and played some weird and wonderful games until about midnight.

The rest of the week we took part in loads of different activities and played games every night. We played crazy golf, high tree tops, pub quiz, went to the pool, tennis, badminton again, roller disco, football pool and more. We also went out to eat a couple of times. I had messaged and called Ian as much as I could but every time I spoke to him he seemed to be mad at me. I tried to explain to him that signal was pretty bad. But that wasn't good enough for him. He thought I was lying. He would never ask about my day and what we had been doing, but I would always ask him about his day. I did my best to make conversation with him but it was useless, he would barely say anything to me, just grumbled down the phone at me. Even my family could see there was something that wasn't quite right. However, I did my best to try and convince them all that everything was fine and I made excuses for him being tired. Every day finished with a phone call to Ian that would upset me, but I hid it well. Once I was off the phone and back to playing games, I would then focus on the games. Each day was better than the last and by the Friday we were all feeling like we didn't want to go home. We had to be checked out by 11am but before we left we were all going out for breakfast. We all sat around the table laughing and talking about our amazing time away. Discussing our favourite parts. We all had pancakes for breakfast and they were fantastic. So light and fluffy. And as we all finished our food we had decided on making this an annual holiday. I already couldn't wait to start booking for next year. After breakfast we went to check out and spend the rest of the day together before heading home later that evening. We were going to a nearby zoo for the day which was only 20 minutes away. When we arrived we parked up and made our way to the entrance. We spent all day looking at all the animals. My favourites were the big cats. They were just so beautiful. My sister loved the monkeys, probably because she is one. My mum and dad loved the elephants and giraffes, respectively. We all had a really lovely day and at the end of the day we went to cosy looking pub for a meal. Our final meal of the holiday, so we were all adamant to make it the best. We sat down at our table and all ordered a drink and started looking through the menu. But we couldn't focus on the menus, we were all too busy laughing. We were the loudest table in the pub but we didn't even realise it. After the waitress came over for the fourth time, we were finally ready to order. We sat and had a wonderful 3 course meal and we stayed sat at our table for a while after we had finished. However, it was soon time to leave which made us all really sad. We didn't want this amazing holiday to end and we didn't know when we would all be together again. So we paid the bill and made our way outside to say our goodbyes. There were more big hugs all round and a few tears, and as we parted ways my heart sank. I was going to miss Tessa and my parents so much.

My mum, dad and I talked about the whole week and laughed together on the drive home. It was dark out now and I knew it would be late by the time I got home. I messaged Ian to say we had just left and I would let him know when we are closer as he was picking me up from a local service station, that was about 30 minutes from where Ian and I lived. The drive home was entertaining in itself, because we got lost for about an hour. Obviously I messaged Ian to let him know I would be later home, but I didn't hear anything back at all. Even from my first message. I didn't pester him, I just guessed he was busy so I waited until we were about an hour away to call him and let him know. When he finally picked up the phone he didn't say much at all.

"Hey, we have just stopped for a quick toilet break, but we are about an hour away." I explained.

"Okay. See you soon. I'll be there in just under an hour." He replied.

I could tell something was wrong but I said that I would see him soon ad we hung up the phone. And as we got back in the car I was actually looking forward to seeing Ian and I couldn't wait to see Daisy. I have to be honest, I was also looking forward to my own bed. When we finally arrived at the service station I could see Ian's car parked up, waiting. We pulled up next to him and I jumped out of the car to go an give him a hug. He got out of his car, slowly and barely said anything to me and didn't hug me back. I instantly knew he was mad, but I didn't know why. I didn't want my parents to leave, but I knew they had to. Then I saw Daisy in the back seat. She was so excited to see me. My parents and I said out goodbyes and gave each other a hug. Ian was already sat in the car with the engine running. I clambered into the car and Daisy was desperate to say 'hello' to me. So I gave her a bit of attention and got her settled so we could make our way home. Ian barely said anything to me. Again, I tried to talk to him but I got nothing back. I had an awful feeling in the pit of my stomach.

Most of the drive home was along country roads and through a couple of little villages. But he drove 70mph the whole way. I was clinging onto the door handle like my life depended on it. He was driving recklessly and dangerously with both me and Daisy in the car. I knew for certain he was mad at me. I was scared but I couldn't say anything to him as it would just make him even more mad. So I just sat there, terrified. And then it happened. He drove over a speed bump, still at 70mph, and lost control. I screamed as I stared at the telegraph pole that we were heading straight for. As we hit it at full force the car bounced backwards to hit the wall that was opposite and bounced forward again. I lost consciousness for only a matter of seconds but when I came round I was in total shock and panic. I heard the hissing of air leaking from the tyre. The airbags didn't go off and I couldn't stop shaking. My first thought was Daisy. As I looked around at her, she looked as terrified as I felt. I tried to calm her down by stroking her. Ian just seemed to be worried about the car and himself. I was so mad that he drove the way he did, putting our lives at risk. Ian then looked at me and asked if I was okay. He got out of the car and walked around it to look at the damage. I slowly pulled on the door handle and carefully stepped out. Then I saw it. The passenger side at the front was badly smashed in. The adrenaline was pumping and my heart felt like it was going a million miles an hour. As I walked around the car I noticed that all the damage was on the passenger side. I was so mad at Ian.

"What on earth have you done!" I shouted with a shaky voice.

"Me? You made me drive like that!" he shouted back.

Suddenly, his attitude changed and he came up to me, tried hugging me and asked I was okay.

"Look, baby, you need to say that you were driving. I had a couple of pints before picking you up." he told me, trying to pass me the keys.

I looked at him in disbelief.

"No way! You were driving, not me!" I said, walking away from him.

He tried his hardest to make it look like I was driving, but I wasn't going to let him put the blame on me. It took hours to get everything sorted. The police arrived and arrested Ian and the car was eventually towed away. I stood at the side of the road for hours once Ian had been taken to the police station, and while the car was being sorted. I was waiting to be taken home for what seemed to be hours. Why did this have to happen? What had I done wrong? Before Ian was taken away by the police he made me say that he had lost control because of the road being wet. I knew that wasn't true and so did the officer. To be honest it all happened so quickly, that I didn't really know what had happened. After about 3 hours Daisy and I finally arrived home, and the first thing I did was fall on the sofa and cry. I was petrified. Ian was with the police somewhere and Daisy and I had to try and process what had happened. After about half an hour I made my way to bed, still crying and with Daisy following me. I knew I wasn't going to sleep I just wanted to be comfortable. I was starting to feel some pain in my side, but I didn't think anything of it. All I wanted was my mum. I just wanted a cuddle from her and then I would know that everything would be ok, but I didn't want to worry her, so I didn't call her.

By the time 4 in the morning rolled round, I still hadn't had any sleep. All of a sudden my phone rang and it was Ian.

"I'm on the way back now. I wont be too long now. How are you?" he asked.

"I'm okay, just my side is really hurting now." I sobbed.

"I won't be long now. I'll explain everything after we have had some sleep." he replied.

I lay there still sobbing and eventually he arrived home. He got into bed and he soon fell asleep. I lay there, wide awake for a long time, not knowing what to do or think. My head was telling me to leave him. But I couldn't leave Daisy alone with him. I didn't know what to do. But it was something I couldn't get out of my head. After thinking about it I decided that this was his last chance. I had given him so many 'last chance's.' But this had to be it now. So, I was going to see how he would treat me over the coming weeks and make a decision from there. Although the thought of trying to make that decision was already scaring me because of the way he had previously tried to guilt me into staying with him. The 3 days after the accident, my side got progressively worse, but so did my breathing. Of course for a while, Ian thought I was over exaggerating or making it all up, but on the fourth day he finally took me to the local minor injuries unit.

"Your chest is sounding a bit crackly, almost like you could have a collapsed lung. We need to get you to hospital to have that confirmed and treated." The nurse explained.

I looked at Ian with a scared look on my face. A collapsed lung? I had gone four days without any sort of medical treatment to then be told I could of had a collapsed lung. I was so scared. I grabbed my bag and coat and we made our way back to the car. We didn't really say anything on the way to the hospital. I just mainly concentrated on breathing and holding on to the door handle as tightly as I possibly could. I was petrified of being in the car with him.

When we arrived at the hospital I started to get really nervous. We pulled into the car park, which was at the bottom of the hill and A and E was at the top. Walking up the hill was slow going and I had to keep stopping. I didn't even make it a quarter of the way up when some nurses came out of a side door and saw my struggling to breathe. They instantly thought in was having an asthma attack, so got me some oxygen and a wheelchair and took me straight to A and E. I had to sit there for about two hours before I was seen and after a chest x-ray, I was finally admitted with a confirmed punctured lung and broken ribs. I was then moved to a ward and a doctor came round to discuss with me how to treat it. Inserting a tube into my side to remove the air. I was told that in 12-24 hours and I should be fine to go home again. Morphine for the pain in my ribs and oxygen. The doctor explained the procedure of putting the tube in and I began to get really nervous. About two hours later I was taken off to a room to have the procedure. Ian waited next to my bed for me and when I got back he helped me back into bed. After having the tube inserted, I had already felt a huge relief. Now it was a matter of waiting to see how long the tube would have to be in. The morphine I was on was making me incredibly sleepy. So it wasn't long before I had fallen asleep. When I woke up Ian was still by my side.

"How you feeling?" he asked.

"I'm doing okay, thank you." I replied, moving my oxygen mask.

"You are going to be here for a little while so I will pop home and pick you up some over night things. Is there anything else you would like my to bring you."

In my sleepy state, I remembered I had a cuddly toy that I got from my last stay in hospital. He was a dog that I called Harlyn. That was the name of the ward that I was on at the time. So I asked Ian to look for my cuddly toy as well for when I was on my own.

"Yes, of course. Not a problem baby." He whispered, as he kissed my forehead.

"I won't be long." he said.

As he left, I felt myself dozing off again and by the time I woke up a few hours later, Ian had returned. He was sat by the side of my bed with everything I had asked for. I could finally change into my pyjamas and get cosy. I kept drifting off to sleep and each time he was there. Then it got to the end of visiting hours and he had to go.

"I will be back tomorrow, okay. Keep me updated with what the doctors say." he said as he gave me a kiss and cuddle goodbye.

Not long after he left, I was given more morphine and the nurses made sure I was okay, and then I fell asleep again. I woke up a lot throughout the night, and hated being there alone, but going on what the doctor had told me earlier, I would be home soon. The nurses were fantastic. They were checking up on me every few hours and making sure I had everything I needed. In the morning they came round to do the morning checks and they gave me some more painkillers and asked what I wanted for breakfast. Once all of that had been sorted, I called my mum and told her everything that had happened in the past few days.

"Oh, honey. How are you feeling now? And is Ian looking after you?" she asked me, concerned.

"Mum, I'm okay. They are looking after me here and he will be back to sit with me soon. I'm sleeping an awful lot anyway. So if he's not here, I'm asleep." I giggled to her.

I could tell she was worried about me and wanted to make sure Ian was looking after me.

"Me and your dad will come and see you tomorrow." she reassured me.

"I should be home by tomorrow, so come over to the house? I'll keep you updated." I replied.

Over the course of the day I spoke to my sister and Ian messaged me plenty before he came to see me. Eventually the doctor came to see me and explained that I would be staying in over night again. I called Ian to explain and he said he would be there as soon as possible. I also called my mum again and told her I would still be in hospital the following day.

"That's okay, we will come up to see you tomorrow afternoon. I'll ring you when we are on our way." she told me.

It made me happy knowing that I would get to see them, even if I didn't really want them seeing me stuck in hospital. I spent pretty much the rest of the day sleeping, and when Ian arrived he sat with me and we talked about his day. I ended up falling asleep again, I just couldn't help it. I was woken up by Ian telling me he would be back the following day. Again, I didn't sleep great through the night, what with being woken up to take painkillers, but I was just glad I had some form of comfort in the form of Harlyn. The following day I napped pretty much until I heard from my mum to say they were on route. I was looking forward to seeing them. When they arrived I sat up in bed and I could see they were upset. They rushed over to give me a hug and afterwards we sat and talked for a while. In the end, though, I did end up falling asleep again. The morphine really was making me so sleepy. And when I woke up again, they were still there. It was so nice to have them there next to me. They could see I was tired so they stayed a little while longer and then left me to sleep some more. Not long after they left, the doctor came round to check on my oxygen levels. He still wasn't happy so he told me that I would be in hospital for a couple more days. All in all I was there for 4 days. When I was finally discharged I was told to keep takin the morphine for the pain of my broken ribs and to take it easy. I was also signed off of work for 2 months. The first 2 weeks after being discharged, Ian was amazing. He helped me with anything that I needed help with. He was sweet and kind. I should of known that it would last.

It had been 3 weeks and I was still in a lot of pain and I was still really sleepy from the morphine. It had obviously been long enough for Ian and I should of been back to being 100% better, but that wasn't he case. One evening in particular, I was lying in bed, on my back as that was the only relatively comfortable position. He clambered into bed next to me and started running his hands over my body.

"No, Ian. I'm in too much pain. Just please let me lie here." I cried.

"Oh, come on. It's been weeks." He pestered.

Was he really going to try it on with me when I was in so much pain? He was the reason that this had happened and all the understanding he'd had, seemed to have vanished.

"This is the only relatively comfortable position for me, please just let me lie here?" I pleaded.

He carried on running his hands all over my body, and I cringed. I moved his hands off of me and that's when he lost his temper. He started shouting but instead of it turning into a massive argument, he rolled over. What I wasn't expecting was him ramming his backside into my hip with such force he hurt me. He didn't say another word and just fell asleep. Luckily he hit my right side, and it was my left side that was injured in the accident. It was at that moment that I finally woke up and realised that I needed to leave him. The problem was, I didn't how I was going to do that. All my savings had disappeared, so it wasn't as simple as just moving out. I had helped Ian out so much with money and I was struggling to build those savings back up again, and he certainly wasn't helping me with that at all. I knew he was going to have to help me, especially seeing as I was off work sick. I spent a couple of days looking for somewhere close by where I could move into on my own, and soon a room in a shared house came up for rent. Now it was time to end the relationship and I was terrified because I knew he would try anything to get me to stay. I had to be strong and stick to my decision. I knew I needed to walk away. So that evening I sat him down and told him that we needed to talk. I was so nervous that I was shaking. I told him everything that was on my mind and I told him that it was over and he instantly burst into tears. He begged and pleaded with me but he didn't listen to anything else I had to say. I also had to try and tell him that I couldn't move out until he agreed to help me, seeing as he had all our money. He didn't say much to that and by the end of the conversation we were both in tears. Because I wouldn't change my mind, Ian stormed off outside. He tried his best to make me feel bad so I would stay with him. But I stayed strong. Once Ian came back inside I told him I was going to head to bed. He just sat there on the sofa and said,

"I can't believe you are throwing this all away!"

A tear rolled down my cheek. I certainly wasn't throwing it all away. He had had countless chances and I couldn't take it anymore. I got into our bed with Daisy next to me and I began crying again. I was going to miss Daisy so much, but I knew I wouldn't of been able to take her with me. The room I had found didn't accept pets. And Ian would never have let me take her. I had to just accept what would happen. Over the next couple of days I went to look at the room with my mum and I decided to take it. The problem was going to be getting the money for the first month's rent. Ian finally agreed to help me move out, but I ended up having to stay in the same house with him for 2 weeks after we had split. The room wasn't going to be ready, and in that 2 weeks while I was waiting Ian tried to convince me to stay with him, even after he had given me the money to help me out. I think he thought that by him doing that, it would make me have a change of heart, and want to stay. Eventually, one Thursday morning, the landlady called me to say I could pick up the keys and start moving my things . I got straight on the phone to my parents to sort out a day that they could come and help me move. They agreed that the following day would be best for everyone so I called my landlady back and arranged a time to meet. Luckily I had most of my things packed in suitcases and boxes, ready to be moved. Ian would also be at work the following day, so I decided to tell him that evening so he knew what was going on. The following morning I got up early and spent some time with Daisy and shockingly Ian was up early too. He took Daisy off and I thought he had gone to work, but he came back a short while later, without Daisy. I was so mad but I just carried on with packing up the last of my things. When he got back he just sat on the sofa, not saying anything.

"Mum and dad will be here soon." I told him, calmly.

"How come?" he asked, bluntly.

"To help me move out." I replied, confused as to why he would ask, when he knew what was going on.

As soon as I said it, he gave me a dirty look and just sat there. I carried on gathering what I could, considering the pain I was in with tears in my eyes and waited for mum and dad to arrive. I still had so much to do but I couldn't help but wonder why he was just sitting on the sofa and hadn't gone to work. When my mum and dad turned up they started taking some of the furniture which was my mum's old furniture, and dropping it off at the shared house. While all of this was happening, Ian just sat there for half the day, not saying anything to anyone. He didn't even have the T.V on. He was just trying to make it awkward for us all. The whole time Ian stayed sat on the sofa, just watching, and because of this, the more and more I thought that I should just stay. It was getting harder and harder to keep walking past him with boxes to go in the car. By early afternoon while Ian was sat in the garden, my mum went out to speak to him. I'm not sure what she told him but she convinced him to stop torturing himself by watching me move all my things out, and to either go to his parents or go to work. He did leave in the end and from what I could gather he went to get Daisy and take her for a walk. We finished packing all my things in peace and move them across, and when we had finally finished loading the last bits into both cars I stood alone in the living room for a moment. I stood and thought back throughout the time we had been together. Reminiscing. For a second, I thought I was doing the wrong thing.

"Maybe I should stay." I whispered to myself.

Then I had that final surge of courage and bravery for that day and I walked outside. Suddenly, my phone pinged,

"When you're done just lock the door. I'm going to my parents for a while." the message read.

I began to cry and as I locked the door I felt a huge weight had been lifted off of my shoulders. I was so scared of what was going to happen next but I knew I had to keep pushing forward. The three of us drove off to the shared house, my new home, and I was thankful that I never told him where I was moving to. When we arrived we unpacked the last of my things from the car and started putting things in place. The next few days I would be putting my own stamp on the place. Mum and dad stayed until early evening to help me. We then decided to get a takeaway for tea. We sat and ate together and had managed to sort a lot of my things. Time was ticking by and I was dreading them both leaving, but I knew that they had too.

"Thank you for all your help." I said, softly.

"It's okay sweetheart. You know we will always help you. We are just glad you are finally out. Now you can finally get yourself in a better place and look after yourself." My dad said, hugging me tightly.

"If you need us for anything at all, just give us a ring, okay? We will be here as soon as we can then. We love you and we are so proud of you!" my mum said with tears in her eyes.

We all hugged and cried together and then they left. I sat in my room, alone and sad. Wondering what to do. I tried not to think about Ian or Daisy, I knew I needed to cut all ties now I had moved out. I just hoped that he would understand that too and not message or call me. However, I woke up in the morning to 5 missed calls and 3 messages from him. I knew instantly by looking at the time that he tried calling, that he would of been drinking. The were all in the early hours of the morning, so I just ignored them. I knew if I replied or called him back he would try to make me feel bad and try to get me to move back with him. Or he would be horrible and say nasty things to me, like he always did when he had been drinking. I knew talking to him would make everything worse. So I didn't reply, I got on with my day. I didn't hear anything else from him during the day so I didn't think much more of it. Until the following morning when I had 7 missed calls, again all early hours. This continued on and off for about 2 months and eventually I couldn't take it anymore so I had to block is number. I knew he was calling me when he was drunk and he would shout and scream at me. I had left him to get away from that. It might of been harsh to just completely ignore him but I just couldn't face the arguing anymore.

After blocking Ian on my phone and all social media, I started to enjoy living alone. There were 3 other rooms in the building I was living in and three lads lived in them. They were decent lads and talking to them took my mind off everything. I thought things were starting to look up, and then the phone calls from a private number began. I never answered any of them but they were constant. They had to be Ian, I was sure of it. Because it was a private number I couldn't block it, so they just kept coming. I just wanted him to leave me alone. In the end I changed my phone number, and finally the calls stopped. I stayed living in the shared house for the next 3 months up until the new year. Hopefully in the new year I could move closer to my parents and then I would feel a lot safer again. By then was a 'time will tell' situation as a the time I couldn't do anything about moving again. In the weeks leading to the new year I was starting to get quite lonely and didn't think I would have any plans, but then I got a call from Nadine.

"Hey, how are you feeling? I hope you're doing okay. How do you feel about a night out? Just me and you, on new years eve? You deserve to let your hair down." she asked me, excitedly.

"Really? That actually sounds amazing. I would love to." I replied, smiling from ear to ear.

"Yay! I can't wait. A proper girly night out!" she genuinely sounded so excited, and so was I.

Over the couple of weeks before new years eve we got everything planned and after Christmas, we started counting down the days to our New Years eve girls night out. We were both so excited.

New years eve finally arrived and Nadine came over to mine and we got ready together and had a couple of drinks before heading out. We had a giggle together and I almost forgot about everything else going on. We took pictures together and had a great time. By about 11pm we left for the club, ready for a night of dancing. Arriving at the club, the queue to get in was pretty long but we knew it was going to be busy, and it was even busier when we eventually got inside. When we did get inside we went straight to the bar and got a couple of drinks. We drank them quickly and made our way to the dancefloor for a dance. We had such a good time, dancing and drinking. And then the DJ made an announcement.

"So, it's almost midnight folks! Time to welcome in the new year. Everyone get to the dancefloor for the countdown to the new year all together! You have 5 minutes!"

Nadine and I looked at each other and found a spot by the DJ booth. It had started getting really crowded and people were still making there way over. Some people stood around the edge of the dancefloor. Nadine grabbed my hands as we danced to the final song of the year and suddenly it cut off and all the T.V screens in the club cut to Big Ben. Everyone started to count down together, all holding hands.

10...9...8...7...6...5...4...3...2...1...

"HAPPY NEW YEAR!!" everyone screamed, loudly.

As the clock struck midnight, the bell chimed and fireworks began. Everyone in the club cheered and started kissing and hugging each other. Nadine looked me dead in the eyes, grabbed both my hands and shouted in my ear over the noise,

"Happy New Year Amanda! Hopefully this will be your year!" and with that we hugged tightly.

Tears rolled down my cheeks. In the middle of the club, finally I felt free. I was finally free of him and hopefully things were about to change! A smile crept across my face, the most genuine smile for a long time and for that moment I was the happiest I have been for a very long time. Now my next chapter could begin.

CPSIA information can be obtained
at www.ICGtesting.com
Printed in the USA
BVHW051925281122
652959BV00001B/27